THE CRICKET IN TIMES SQUARE

OTHER YEARLING BOOKS YOU WILL ENJOY:

YEARLING BOOKS/YOUNG YEARLINGS/YEARLING CLASSICS are designed especially to entertain and enlighten young people. Patricia Reilly Giff, consultant to this series, received her bachelor's degree from Marymount College and a master's degree in history from St. John's University. She holds a Professional Diploma in Reading and a Doctorate of Humane Letters from Hofstra University. She was a teacher and reading consultant for many years, and is the author of numerous books for young readers.

For a complete listing of all Yearling titles, write to
Dell Readers Service,
P.O. Box 1045,
South Holland, IL 60473.

GEORGE SELDEN

The
Cricket
in Times Square

ILLUSTRATED BY

Garth Williams

A YEARLING BOOK

Published by
Bantam Doubleday Dell Books for Young Readers
a division of
Bantam Doubleday Dell Publishing Group, Inc.
1540 Broadway
New York, New York 10036

ISBN: 0-440-22022-X

Reprinted by arrangement with Farrar, Straus and Giroux

Printed in the United States of America

One Previous Edition

10 9 8 7 6 5 4 3 2 1

OPM

CONTENTS

ONE

Tucker

A mouse was looking at Mario.

The mouse's name was Tucker, and he was sitting in the opening of an abandoned drain pipe in the subway station at Times Square. The drain pipe was his home. Back a few feet in the wall, it opened out into a pocket that Tucker had filled with the bits of paper and shreds of cloth he collected. And when he wasn't collecting, "scrounging" as he called it, or sleeping, he liked to sit at the opening of the drain pipe and watch the world go by—at least as much of the world as hurried through the Times Square subway station.

Tucker finished the last few crumbs of a cookie he was eating—a Lorna Doone shortbread he had found earlier in the evening—and licked off his whiskers. "Such a pity," he sighed.

Every Saturday night now for almost a year he had watched Mario tending his father's newsstand. On weekdays, of course, the boy had to get to bed early, but over the weekends Papa Bellini let him take his part in helping out with the family business. Far into the night Mario waited. Papa hoped that by staying open as late as possible his newsstand might get some of the business that would otherwise have gone to the larger stands. But there wasn't much business tonight.

"The poor kid might as well go home," murmured Tucker Mouse to himself. He looked around the station.

The bustle of the day had long since subsided, and even the nighttime crowds, returning from the theaters and movies, had vanished. Now and then a person or two would come down one of the many stairs that led from the street and dart through the station. But at this hour everyone was in a hurry to get to bed. On the lower level the trains were running much less often. There would be a long stretch of silence; then the mounting roar as a string of cars approached Times Square; then a pause while it let off old passengers and took on new ones; and finally the rush of sound as it disappeared up the dark tunnel. And the hush fell again. There was an emptiness in the air. The whole station seemed to be waiting for the crowds of people it needed.

Tucker Mouse looked back at Mario. He was sitting on a three legged stool behind the counter of the newsstand. In front of him all the magazines and newspapers were displayed as neatly as he knew how to

make them. Papa Bellini had made the newsstand himself many years ago. The space inside was big enough
for Mario, but Mama and Papa were cramped when
they each took their turn. A shelf ran along one side,
and on it were a little secondhand radio, a box of
Kleenex (for Mama's hay fever), a box of kitchen
matches (for lighting Papa's pipe), a cash register
(for money—which there wasn't much of), and an
alarm clock (for no good reason at all). The cash register had one drawer, which was always open. It had
gotten stuck once, with all the money the Bellinis had
in the world inside it, so Papa decided it would be
safer never to shut it again. When the stand was closed
for the night, the money that was left there to start off
the new day was perfectly safe, because Papa had also
made a big wooden cover, with a lock, that fitted over
the whole thing.

Mario had been listening to the radio. He switched
it off. Way down the tracks he could see the lights of
the shuttle train coming towards him. On the level
of the station where the newsstand was, the only tracks
were the ones on which the shuttle ran. That was a
short train that went back and forth from Times
Square to Grand Central, taking people from the sub-
ways on the east side of New York City over to the
lines on the west. Mario knew most of the conductors
on the shuttle. They all liked him and came over to
talk between trips.

The Cricket in Times Square

The train screeched to a stop beside the newsstand, blowing a gust of hot air in front of it. Only nine or ten people got out. Tucker watched anxiously to see if any of them stopped to buy a paper.

"All late papers!" shouted Mario as they hurried by. "Magazines!"

No one stopped. Hardly anyone even looked at him. Mario sank back on his stool. All evening long he had only sold fifteen papers and four magazines. In the drain pipe Tucker Mouse, who had been keeping count too, sighed and scratched his ear.

Mario's friend Paul, a conductor on the shuttle, came over to the stand. "Any luck?" he asked.

"No," said Mario. "Maybe on the next train."

"There's going to be less and less until morning," said Paul.

Mario rested his chin on the palm of his hand. "I can't understand it," he said. "It's Saturday night too. Even the Sunday papers aren't going."

Paul leaned up against the newsstand. "You're up awfully late tonight," he said.

"Well, I can sleep on Sundays," said Mario. "Besides, school's out now. Mama and Papa are picking me up on the way home. They went to visit some friends. Saturday's the only chance they have."

Over a loud speaker came a voice saying, "Next train for Grand Central, track two."

" 'Night, Mario," Paul said. He started off toward

the shuttle. Then he stopped, reached in his pocket and flipped a half dollar over the counter. Mario caught the big coin. "I'll take a Sunday *Times*," Paul said, and picked up the newspaper.

"Hey wait!" Mario called after him. "It's only twenty-five cents. You've got a quarter coming."

But Paul was already in the car. The door slid closed. He smiled and waved through the window. With a lurch the train moved off, its lights glimmering away through the darkness.

Tucker Mouse smiled too. He liked Paul. In fact he liked anybody who was nice to Mario. But it was late now: time to crawl back to his comfortable niche in the wall and go to sleep. Even a mouse who lives in the subway station in Times Square has to sleep sometimes. And Tucker had a big day planned for tomorrow, collecting things for his home and snapping up bits of food that fell from the lunch counters all over the station. He was just about to turn into the drain pipe when he heard a very strange sound.

Now Tucker Mouse had heard almost all the sounds that can be heard in New York City. He had heard the rumble of subway trains and the shriek their iron wheels make when they go around a corner. From above, through the iron grills that open onto the streets, he had heard the thrumming of the rubber tires of automobiles, and the hooting of their horns, and the howling of their brakes. And he had heard the babble of voices when the station was full of human beings, and the barking of the dogs that some of them had on leashes. Birds, the pigeons of New York, and cats, and even the high purring of airplanes above the city Tucker had heard. But in all his days, and on all his journeys through the greatest city in the world, Tucker had never heard a sound quite like this one.

TWO

Mario

Mario heard the sound too. He stood up and listened intently. The noise of the shuttle rattled off into silence. From the streets above came the quiet murmur of the late traffic. There was a noise of rustling nothingness in the station. Still Mario listened, straining to catch the mysterious sound. . . . And there it came again.

It was like a quick stroke across the strings of a violin, or like a harp that had been plucked suddenly. If a leaf in a green forest far from New York had fallen at midnight through the darkness into a thicket, it might have sounded like that.

Mario thought he knew what it was. The summer before he had gone to visit a friend who lived on Long Island. One afternoon, as the low sun reached long yellow fingers through the tall grass, he had stopped beside a meadow to listen to just such a noise. But there had been many of them then—a chorus. Now there was only one. Faintly it came again through the subway station.

9

The Cricket in Times Square

Mario slipped out of the newsstand and stood wait-ing. The next time he heard the sound, he went to-ward it. It seemed to come from one corner, next to the stairs that led up to Forty-second Street. Softly Mario went toward the spot. For several minutes there was only the whispering silence. Whatever it was that was making the sound had heard him coming and was quiet. Silently Mario waited. Then he heard it again, rising from a pile of waste papers and soot that had blown against the concrete wall.

He went down and very gently began to lift off the papers. One by one he inspected them and laid them to one side. Down near the bottom the papers became dirtier and dirtier. Mario reached the floor. He began to feel with his hands through the dust and soot. And wedged in a crack under all the refuse, he found what he'd been looking for.

It was a little insect, about an inch long and covered with dirt. It had six legs, two long antennae on its head and what seemed to be a pair of wings folded on its back. Holding his discovery as carefully as his fin-gers could, Mario lifted the insect up and rested him in the palm of his hand.

"A cricket!" he exclaimed.

Keeping his cupped hand very steady, Mario walked back to the newsstand. The cricket didn't move. And he didn't make that little musical noise any more. He

just lay perfectly still—as if he were sleeping, or frightened to death.

Mario pulled out a tissue of Kleenex and laid the cricket on it. Then he took another and started to dust him off. Ever so softly he tapped the hard black shell, and the antennae, and legs, and wings. Gradually the dirt that had collected on the insect fell away. His true color was still black, but now it had a bright, glossy sheen.

When Mario had cleaned off the cricket as much as he could, he hunted around the floor of the station for a matchbox. In a minute he'd found one and knocked out one end. Then he folded a sheet of Kleenex, tucked it in the box and put the cricket in. It made a perfect bed. The cricket seemed to like his new home. He moved around a few times and settled himself comfortably.

Mario sat for a time, just looking. He was so happy and excited that when anyone walked through the station, he forgot to shout "Newspapers!" and "Magazines!"

Then a thought occured to him: perhaps the cricket was hungry. He rummaged through his jacket pocket and found a piece of a chocolate bar that had been left over from supper. Mario broke off one corner and held it out to the cricket on the end of his finger. Cautiously the insect lifted his head to the chocolate. He seemed to smell it a moment, then took a bit. A shiver of pleasure went over Mario as the cricket ate from his hand.

Mama and Papa Bellini came up the stairs from the lower level of the station. Mama was a short woman— a little stouter than she liked to admit—who wheezed and got a red face when she had to climb steps. Papa was tall and somewhat bent over, but he had a kindness that shone about him. There seemed always to be something smiling inside Papa. Mario was so busy feeding his cricket that he didn't see them when they came up to the newsstand.

"So?" said Mama, craning over the counter. "What now?"

"I found a cricket!" Mario exclaimed. He picked the insect up very gently between his thumb and forefinger and held him out for his parents to see.

Mama studied the little black creature carefully. "It's a bug," she pronounced finally. "Throw it away."

Mario's happiness fell in ruins. "No, Mama," he said anxiously. "Its a special kind of bug. Crickets are good luck."

"Good luck, ay?" Mama's voice had a way of sounding very dry when she didn't believe something. "Cricketers are good luck—so I suppose ants are better luck. And cockroaches are the best luck of all. Throw it away."

"Please, Mama, I want to keep him for a pet."

13

Mario

"No bugs are coming to my house," said Mama. "We've got enough already with the screens full of holes. He'll whistle to his friends—they'll come from all over—we'll have a houseful of cricketers."

"No we won't," said Mario in a low voice. "I'll fix the screens." But he knew it was no use arguing with Mama. When she had made up her mind, you might as well try to reason with the Eighth Avenue subway.

"How was selling tonight?" asked Papa. He was a peaceful man and always tried to head off arguments. Changing the subject was something he did very well.

"Fifteen papers and four magazines," said Mario. "And Paul just bought a Sunday *Times*."

"No one took a *Musical America*, or anything else nice?" Papa was very proud that his newsstand carried all of what he called the "quality magazines."

"No," answered Mario.

"So you spend less time playing with cricketers, you'll sell more papers," said Mama.

"Oh now, now," Papa soothed her. "Mario couldn't help it if nobody buys."

"You can tell the temperature with crickets too," said Mario. "You count the number of chirps in a minute, divide by four and add forty. They're very intelligent."

"Who needs a cricketer-thermometer?" said Mama. "It's coming on summer, it's New York—it's hot. And

The Cricket in Times Square

how do you know so much about cricketers. Are you one?"

"Jimmy Lebovski told me last summer," said Mario.

"Then give it to the expert Jimmy Lebovski," said Mama. "Bugs carry germs. He doesn't come in the house."

Mario looked down at his new friend in the palm of his hand. Just for once he had been really happy. The cricket seemed to know that something was wrong. He jumped onto the shelf and crept into the match-box.

"He could keep it here in the newsstand," suggested Papa.

Mario jumped at that idea. "Yes, and then he wouldn't have to come home. I could feed him here, and leave him here, and you'd never have to see him," he said to Mama. "And when you took the stand, I'd bring him with me."

Mama paused. "Cricketer," she said scornfully. "What do we want with a cricketer?"

"What do we want with a newsstand?" said Papa. "We got it—let's keep it." There was something re-signed, but nice, about Papa.

"You said I could have a dog," said Mario, "but I never got him. And I never got a cat, or a bird, or any-thing. I wanted this cricket for my pet."

"He's yours then," said Papa. And when Papa spoke

16

in a certain quiet tone— that was all there was to it. Even Mama didn't dare disagree.

She took a deep breath. "Oh well—" she sighed. And Mario knew it would be all right. Mama's saying "oh well" was her way of giving in. "But only on trial he stays. At the first sign of the cricketer friends, or if we come down with peculiar diseases—out he goes!"

"Yes, Mama, anything you say," said Mario.

"Come on, Mario," Papa said. "Help me close up."

Mario held the matchbox up to his eye. He was sure the cricket looked much happier, now that he could stay. "Goodnight," he said. "I'll be back in the morning."

"Talking to it yet!" said Mama. "I've got a cricketer for a son."

Papa took one side of the cover to the newsstand, Mario the other, and together they fitted it on. Papa locked it down. As they were going downstairs to the trains, Mario looked back over his shoulder. He could almost feel the cricket, snugged away in his matchbox bed, in the darkness.

THREE

Chester

Tucker Mouse had been watching the Bellinis and listening to what they said. Next to scrounging, eavesdropping on human beings was what he enjoyed most. That was one of the reasons he lived in the Times Square subway station. As soon as the family disappeared, he darted out across the floor and scooted up to the newsstand. At one side the boards had separated and there was a wide space he could jump through. He'd been in a few times before—just exploring. For a moment he stood under the three legged stool, letting his eyes get used to the darkness. Then he jumped up on it.

"Psst!" he whispered. "Hey you up there—are you awake?"

There was no answer.

"Psst! Psst! Hey!" Tucker whispered again, louder this time.

From the shelf above came a scuffling, like little feet feeling their way to the edge. "Who is that going 'psst'?" said a voice.

The Cricket in Times Square

"It's me," said Tucker. "Down here on the stool."

A black head, with two shiny black eyes, peered down at him. "Who are you?"

"A mouse," said Tucker, "Who are *you*?"

"I'm Chester Cricket," said the cricket. He had a high, musical voice. Everything he said seemed to be spoken to an unheard melody.

"My name's Tucker," said Tucker Mouse. "Can I come up?"

"I guess so," said Chester Cricket. "This isn't my house anyway."

Tucker jumped up beside the cricket and looked him all over. "A cricket," he said admiringly. "So you're a cricket. I never saw one before."

"I've seen mice before," the cricket said. "I knew quite a few back in Connecticut."

"Is that where you're from?" asked Tucker.

"Yes," said Chester. "I guess I'll never see it again," he added wistfully.

"How did you get to New York?" asked Tucker Mouse.

"It's a long story," sighed the cricket.

"Tell me," said Tucker, settling back on his haunches. He loved to hear stories. It was almost as much fun as eavesdropping—if the story was true.

"Well it must have been two—no, three days ago," Chester Cricket began. "I was sitting on top of my stump, just enjoying the weather and thinking how nice it was that summer had started. I live inside an old tree stump, next to a willow tree, and I often go up to the roof to look around. And I'd been practicing jumping that day too. On the other side of the stump from the willow tree there's a brook that runs past, and I'd been jumping back and forth across it to get my legs in condition for the summer. I do a lot of jumping, you know."

"Me too," said Tucker Mouse. "Especially around the rush hour."

"And I had just finished jumping when I smelled something," Chester went on, "liverwurst, which I love."

"You like liverwurst?" Tucker broke in. "Wait! Wait! Just wait!"

In one leap, he sprang down all the way from the shelf to the floor and dashed over to his drain pipe. Chester shook his head as he watched him go. He thought Tucker was a very excitable person—even for a mouse.

Inside the drain pipe, Tucker's nest was a jumble of papers, scraps of cloth, buttons, lost jewelry, small change, and everything else that can be picked up in a subway station. Tucker tossed things left and right in a wild search. Neatness was not one of the things he aimed at in life. At last he discovered what he was looking for: a big piece of liverwurst he had found earlier that evening. It was meant to be for breakfast tomorrow, but he decided that meeting his first cricket was a special occasion. Holding the liverwurst between his teeth, he whisked back to the newsstand.

"Look!" he said proudly, dropping the meat in front of Chester Cricket. "Liverwurst! You continue the story—we'll enjoy a snack too."

"That's very nice of you," said Chester. He was touched that a mouse he had known only a few minutes would share his food with him. "I had a little chocolate before, but besides that, nothing for three days."

"Eat! Eat!" said Tucker. He bit the liverwurst into two pieces and gave Chester the bigger one. "So you smelled the liverwurst—then what happened?"

"I hopped down from the stump and went off toward the smell," said Chester.

"Very logical," said Tucker Mouse, munching with his cheeks full. "Exactly what I would have done."

"It was coming from a picnic basket," said Chester. "A couple of tuffets away from my stump the meadow begins, and there was a whole bunch of people having a picnic. They had hard boiled eggs, and cold roast chicken, and roast beef, and a whole lot of other things besides the liverwurst sandwiches, which I smelled."

Tucker Mouse moaned with pleasure at the thought of all that food.

"They were having such a good time laughing and singing songs that they didn't notice me when I jumped

into the picnic basket," continued Chester. "I was sure they wouldn't mind if I had just a taste."

"Naturally not," said Tucker Mouse sympathetically. "Why mind? Plenty for all. Who could blame you?"

"Now I have to admit," Chester went on, "I had more than a taste. As a matter of fact, I ate so much that I couldn't keep my eyes open—what with being tired from the jumping and everything. And I fell asleep right there in the picnic basket. The first thing I knew, somebody had put a bag on top of me that had the last of the roast beef sandwiches in it. I couldn't move!"

"Imagine!" Tucker exclaimed. "Trapped under roast beef sandwiches! Well, there are worse fates."

"At first I wasn't too frightened," said Chester. "After all, I thought, they probably come from New Canaan or some other nearby town. They'll have to unpack the basket sooner or later. Little did I know!" He shook his head and sighed. "I could feel the basket being carried into a car and riding somewhere and then being lifted down. That must have been the railroad station. Then I went up again and there was a rattling and roaring sound, the way a train makes. By this time I was pretty scared. I knew every minute was taking me further away from my stump, but there wasn't anything I could do. I was getting awfully cramped too, under those roast beef sandwiches."

Chester

"Didn't you try to eat your way out?" asked Tucker.

"I didn't have any room," said Chester. "But every now and then the train would give a lurch and I managed to free myself a little. We traveled on and on, and then the train stopped. I didn't have any idea where we were, but as soon as the basket was carried off, I could tell from the noise it must be New York."

"You never were here before?" Tucker asked.

"Goodness no!" said Chester. "But I've heard about it. There was a swallow I used to know who told about flying over New York every spring and fall on her way to the North and back. But what would I be doing here?" He shifted uneasily from one set of legs to another. "I'm a country cricket."

"Don't worry," said Tucker Mouse. "I'll feed you liverwurst. You'll be all right. Go on with the story."

"It's almost over," said Chester. "The people got off one train and walked a ways and got on another— even noisier than the first."

"Must have been the subway," said Tucker.

"I guess so," Chester Cricket said. "You can imagine how scared I was. I didn't know *where* I was going! For all I knew they could have been heading for Texas, although I don't guess many people from Texas come all the way to Connecticut for a picnic."

"It could happen," said Tucker, nodding his head.

"Anyway I worked furiously to get loose. And finally I made it. When they got off the second train, I took a flying leap and landed in a pile of dirt over in the corner of this place where we are."

"Such an introduction to New York," said Tucker, "to land in a pile of dirt in the Times Square subway station. Tsk, tsk, tsk."

"And here I am," Chester concluded forlornly. "I've been lying over there for three days not knowing what to do. At last I got so nervous I began to chirp."

"That was the sound!" interrupted Tucker Mouse. "I heard it, but I didn't know what it was."

"Yes, that was me," said Chester. "Usually I don't chirp until later on in the summer—but my goodness, I had to do *something*!"

The cricket had been sitting next to the edge of the shelf. For some reason—perhaps it was a faint noise, like padded feet tiptoeing across the floor—he happened to look down. A shadowy form that had been crouching silently below in the darkness made a spring and landed right next to Tucker and Chester.

"Watch out!" Chester shouted, "A cat!" He dove headfirst into the matchbox.

FOUR

Harry Cat

Chester buried his head in the Kleenex. He didn't
want to see his new friend, Tucker Mouse, get killed.
Back in Connecticut he had sometimes watched the
one-sided fights of cats and mice in the meadow, and
unless the mice were near their holes, the fights always ended in the same way. But this cat had been
upon them too quickly: Tucker couldn't have escaped.

There wasn't a sound. Chester lifted his head and
very cautiously looked behind him. The cat—a huge
tiger cat with gray-green and black stripes along his
body—was sitting on his hind legs, switching his tail
around his forepaws. And directly between those forepaws, in the very jaws of his enemy, sat Tucker Mouse.
He was watching Chester curiously. The cricket began
to make frantic signs that the mouse should look up
and see what was looming over him.

Very casually Tucker raised his head. The cat looked
straight down on him. "Oh him," said Tucker, chuck-
ing the cat under the chin with his right front paw,

27

"he's my best friend. Come out from the matchbox."

Chester crept out, looking first at one, then the other.

"Chester, meet Harry Cat," said Tucker. "Harry, this is Chester. He's a cricket."

"I'm very pleased to make your acquaintance," said Harry Cat in a silky voice.

"Hello," said Chester. He was sort of ashamed because of all the fuss he'd made. "I wasn't scared for myself. But I thought cats and mice were enemies."

"In the country, maybe," said Tucker. "But in New York we gave up those old habits long ago. Harry is my oldest friend. He lives with me over in the drain pipe. So how was scrounging tonight, Harry?"

"Not so good," said Harry Cat. "I was over in the ash cans on the East Side, but those rich people don't throw out as much garbage as they should."

"Chester, make that noise again for Harry," said Tucker Mouse.

Chester lifted the black wings that were carefully folded across his back and with a quick, expert stroke drew the top one over the bottom. A "thrumm" echoed through the station.

"Lovely—very lovely," said the cat. "This cricket has talent."

"I thought it was singing," said Tucker. "But you do it like playing a violin, with one wing on the other?"

"Yes," said Chester. "These wings aren't much good for flying, but I prefer music anyhow." He made three rapid chirps.

Tucker Mouse and Harry Cat smiled at each other. "It makes me want to purr to hear it," said Harry.

"Some people say a cricket goes 'chee chee chee,'" explained Chester. "And others say, 'treet treet treet,' but we crickets don't think it sounds like either one of those."

"It sounds to me as if you were going 'crik crik crik,'" said Harry.

"Maybe that's why they call him a 'cricket,'" said Tucker.

They all laughed. Tucker had a squeaky laugh that sounded as if he were hiccuping. Chester was feeling much happier now. The future did not seem nearly as gloomy as it had over in the pile of dirt in the corner.

"Are you going to stay a while in New York?" asked Tucker.

"I guess I'll have to," said Chester. "I don't know how to get home."

"Well, we could always take you to Grand Central Station and put you on a train going back to Connecticut," said Tucker. "But why don't you give the city a try. Meet new people—see new things. Mario likes you very much."

"Yes, but his mother doesn't," said Chester. "She thinks I carry germs."

Harry Cat

"Germs!" said Tucker scornfully. "She wouldn't know a germ if one gave her a black eye. Pay no attention."

"Too bad you couldn't have found more successful friends," said Harry Cat. "I fear for the future of this newsstand."

"It's true," echoed Tucker sadly. "They're going broke fast." He jumped up on a pile of magazines and read off the names in the half light that slanted through the cracks in the wooden cover "*Art News—Musical America*. Who would read them but a few long-hairs?"

"I don't understand the way you talk," said Chester. Back in the meadow he had listened to bullfrogs, and woodchucks, and rabbits, even a few snakes, but he had never heard anyone speak like Tucker Mouse. "What is a long-hair?"

Tucker scratched his head and thought a moment. "A long-hair is an extra refined person," he said. "You take an Afghan Hound—that's a long-hair."

"Do Afghan Hounds read *Musical America*?" asked the cricket.

'They would if they could," said Tucker.

Chester shook his head. "I'm afraid I won't get along in New York," he said.

"Oh sure you will!" squeaked Tucker Mouse. "Harry, suppose we take Chester up and show him Times Square. Would you like that, Chester?"

"I guess so," said Chester, although he was really a little leery of venturing out into New York City.

31

The Cricket in Times Square

The three of them jumped down to the floor. The crack in the side of the newsstand was just wide enough for Harry to get through. As they crossed the station floor, Tucker pointed out the local sights of interest, such as the Nedick's lunch counter—Tucker spent a lot of time around there—and the Loft's candy store. Then they came to the drain pipe. Chester had to make short little hops to keep from hitting his head as they went up. There seemed to be hundreds of twistings and turnings, and many other pipes that opened off the main route, but Tucker Mouse knew his way perfectly—even in the dark. At last Chester saw light above them. One more hop brought him out onto the sidewalk. And there he gasped, holding his breath and crouching against the cement.

They were standing at one corner of the Times building, which is at the south end of Times Square. Above the cricket, towers that seemed like mountains of light rose up into the night sky. Even this late the neon signs were still blazing. Reds, blues, greens and yellows flashed down on him. And the air was full of the roar of traffic and the hum of human beings. It was as if Times Square were a kind of shell, with colors and noises breaking in great waves inside it. Chester's heart hurt him and he closed his eyes. The sight was too terrible and beautiful for a cricket who up to now had measured high things by the height of

32

his willow tree and sounds by the burble of a running brook.

"How do you like it?" asked Tucker Mouse.

"Well—it's—it's quite something," Chester stuttered.

"You should see it New Year's Eve," said Harry Cat.

Gradually Chester's eyes got used to the lights. He looked up. And way far above them, above New York, and above the whole world, he made out a star that he knew was a star he used to look at back in Connecticut. When they had gone down to the station and Chester was in the matchbox again, he thought about that star. It made him feel better to think that there was one familiar thing, twinkling above him, amidst so much that was new and strange.

FIVE

Sunday Morning

The next morning Mario came back to the newsstand with his father. Usually he slept late on Sunday,
but today he was up before either of his parents and
kept urging Papa Bellini to hurry.

They lifted off the cover and Mario dashed inside.
He held up the matchbox and looked in. There was
Chester, lying on the Kleenex. The cricket wasn't
asleep though—he had been waiting for Mario. He
chirped once.

Papa smiled when he heard the chirp. "He must like
it here," he said. "He didn't run away in the night."

"I knew he wouldn't," said Mario.

For breakfast Mario had brought a crust of bread,
a lump of sugar and a cold brussel sprout. He wasn't
quite sure what crickets liked, so he decided to try him
out on everything. Chester jumped over Mario's little
finger into the palm of his hand where the food was.
Back in the meadow his usual diet was leaves and grass,
and every now and then a piece of tender bark, but

The Cricket in Times Square

here in New York he was eating bread and candy and liverwurst, and finding them very tasty at that.

When Chester had had as much as he wanted, Mario wrapped what was left in a piece of wax paper and put it inside the cash register. Then he slipped the cricket back inside the matchbox and took him over to one of the lunch counters.

"Look," he said to the counterman. "This is my new pet. He's a cricket."

The counterman's name was Mickey. He had red, curly hair. "That's a fine cricket," he said, peering in at Chester.

"May he have a glass of water, please?" asked Mario.

Mickey said, "Sure," and gave him the glass. Mario held Chester by the hind legs and lowered him carefully until his head was just above the water. Chester dunked his head in and had a big drink. Then he pulled it out, took a breath and went in for another.

"Why don't you let him stand on the rim?" said Mickey. He was very interested in watching Chester, since he had never seen a cricket drinking from a glass before.

Mario set his pet on the edge of the glass and gently drew his hand away. Chester bent down to try to reach the water. But the glass was too slippery. He toppled in. Mario hauled him out and dried him off with a paper napkin. But Chester didn't mind the dunking. He had fallen in the brook a couple of times back in

36

The Cricket in Times Square

Connecticut. And he knew it would take him a while to get used to city life—like drinking out of glasses.

"How would the cricket like a soda?" asked Mickey.

"Very much, I think," said Mario.

"What flavor?" Mickey asked.

Mario thought a minute. "Strawberry, I guess," he answered. That happened to be his own favorite flavor.

Mickey took a table spoon and put a drop of strawberry syrup into it. Then he added a drop of cream, a squirt of soda water and a dip of ice cream about as big as your fingernail. That is how you make a cricket's strawberry soda. He also made one for Mario—a little larger than Chester's, but not too big, because it was free.

When the sodas were gone, Mickey took a paper cup and wrote CRICKET on it. "This is his own cup," he said to Mario. "You can come over and get fresh water any time."

"Thanks, Mickey," said Mario. He put Chester back in the matchbox. "I've got to go to get him a house now."

"Bring him back soon." Mickey called after them. "I'll make him a sundae too."

At the newsstand Papa Bellini was talking to Mr. Smedley. Mr. Smedley was the best customer the Bellinis had. He was a music teacher who came to buy *Musical America* at ten-thirty in the morning on the last Sunday of every month, on his way home from church. No matter what the weather was like, he always carried a long, neatly rolled umbrella. As usual, Papa and Mr. Smedley had been talking about opera. More than anything else the Bellini family liked Italian opera. Every Saturday during the winter, when the opera was broadcast, they would sit clustered around the radio in the newsstand, straining to hear the music above the din of the subway station.

"Good morning, Mr. Smedley," said Mario. "Guess what I have."

Mr. Smedley couldn't guess.

"A cricket!" said Mario, and held Chester up for the music teacher to see.

"How delightful!" said Mr. Smedley. "What an enchanting little creature."

"Do you want to hold him?" asked Mario.

Mr. Smedley shrank back. "Oh I don't think so," he said. "I was stung by a bee when I was eight years old, and since then I've been a little timid about insects."

"He won't sting you," said Mario. He tipped the matchbox up and Chester fell out in Mr. Smedley's hand. It made the music teacher shiver to feel him. "I heard him chirping last night," said Mario.

"Do you think he'd chirp for me?" asked Mr. Smedley.

"Maybe," said Mario. He put Chester on the counter and said, "Chirp, please." Then, so Chester couldn't misunderstand, he made a chirping noise himself. It didn't sound much like a cricket, but Chester got the idea. He uncrossed his wings and made a real chirp.

Papa and Mr. Smedley exclaimed with delight. "That was a perfect middle C," said Mr. Smedley. He raised his hand like an orchestra conductor, and when he lowered it, Chester chirped on the downbeat.

"Do you want to give him music lessons, Mr. Smedley?" asked Mario.

"What could I teach him?" said Mr. Smedley. "He's already been taught by the greatest teacher of all, Mario—Nature herself. She gave him his wings to rub together and the instinct to make such lovely sounds. I could add nothing to the genius of this little black Orpheus."

"Who is Orpheus, Mr. Smedley?" asked Mario.

"Orpheus was the greatest musician who ever lived," said the music teacher. "Long, long ago he played on a harp—and he played it so beautifully that not only human beings, but animals and even the rocks and trees and waterfalls stopped their work to listen to him. The lion left off chasing the deer, the rivers paused in their courses, and the wind held its breath. The whole world was silent."

Mario didn't know what to say. He liked that picture of everyone keeping quiet to listen. "That must have been awfully good playing," he said finally.

Mr. Smedley smiled. "It was," he said. "Perhaps

Sunday Morning

some day your cricket will play as well. I prophesy great things for a creature of such ability, Mario."

"You hear?" said Papa Bellini. "He could be famous, maybe."

Mario heard, all right. And he remembered what Mr. Smedley had said later on that summer. But right now he had other things on his mind. "Papa, can I go down to Chinatown and get my cricket a house?" he asked.

"A house? What kind of a house?" said his father.

"Jimmy Lebovski said that the Chinese like crickets very much, and they build special cages for them," Mario explained.

"It's Sunday," said Papa. "There won't be any stores open."

"Well but there may be one or two open," said Mario. "It's Chinatown—and besides, I could see where to go later on."

"All right, Mario," Papa Bellini began, "but—"

But Mario wasn't waiting for any "buts." He scooped Chester into the matchbox, shouted "Good-bye, Mr. Smedley" over his shoulder and headed for the stairway leading to the downtown subway trains. Papa and Mr. Smedley watched him go. Then Papa turned to the music teacher with a happy, hopeless expression on his face, shrugged his shoulders and the two of them began talking about opera again.

41

SIX

Sai Fong

Mario took the IRT local subway downtown. He held the matchbox up at the level of his chest so the cricket could see out. This was the first time Chester had been able to watch where he was going on the subway. The last time he had been buried under roast beef sandwiches. He hung out of the box, gazing up and down the car. Chester was a curious cricket and as long as he was here in New York, he meant to see as much as he could.

He was staring at an old lady wearing a straw hat, wondering if the flowers on it were real, and if they were what they would taste like, when the train lurched to a halt. Like most people who first ride the subway, Chester wasn't used to the abrupt stops. He toppled out of the matchbox, into Mario's lap.

The boy picked him up again. "You've got to be

43

careful," he said, putting his finger over the open end of the box so there was just enough room for Chester to poke his head out.

At the Canal street stop Mario got off and walked over several blocks to Chinatown. Chester craned his head out as far as he could to get his first look at New York by day. The buildings in this part of town weren't nearly as high as they were in Times Square, but they were still high enough to make Chester Cricket feel very small.

In Chinatown, as Papa had said, all the shops were closed. Mario walked up and down the narrow, curving streets, zig-zagging across them so he could look in the windows on both sides. In some he saw the cardboard shells that open up into beautiful paper flowers if you put them in a glass of water, and in others the glass wind harps that tinkle when they're hung in the window where the breeze can reach them. But he couldn't find a cricket cage anywhere.

Down at the end of an alley there was an especially old shop. The paint was peeling off the doors and the windows were crammed with years' and years' collection of knickknacks. A sign hanging out in front said, "SAI FONG—CHINESE NOVELTIES." and printed underneath, in smaller letters, was "also do hand laundry." Sitting cross-legged on the doorstep was an old Chinese man. He was wearing a silk vest over his shirt with dragons embroidered on it in red thread, and he was smoking a long white clay pipe.

Mario stopped and looked in the shop window. The old Chinese man didn't turn his head, but he looked slyly at the boy out of the corner of his eyes. Slowly he drew the pipe out of his mouth and blew a puff of smoke into the air.

"Are you Mr. Fong?" asked Mario.

The man smoothly twisted his head, as if it were on a pivot, and looked at Mario. "I Sai Fong," he answered. His voice sounded as high and dry as a cricket's chirping.

"I would like to buy a cricket cage, if you have any," said Mario.

Sai Fong put the pipe back in his mouth and took a few puffs. His eyes became even narrower than they had been before. "You got clicket?" he asked finally in a voice so soft that Mario could hardly hear it.

"Yes," said Mario. "Here he is." He opened the matchbox. Chester and Sai Fong looked at each other.

"Oh velly good!" said Sai Fong, and a remarkable change came over him. He suddenly became very lively, almost dancing a jig on the sidewalk. "You got clicket! Eee hee hee! Velly good! You got clicket! Hee hee!" He was laughing delightedly.

Mario was startled by Sai Fong's quick change. "I want to get him a house," he said.

45

The Cricket in Times Square

"Come in shop, please," said Sai Fong. He opened the door and they both went in.

Mario had never seen such a cluttered room. It was a jumble of Chinese odds and ends. Everything from silk kimonos to chop sticks to packages of hand laundry littered the shelves and chairs. And there was a faint, sweet smell of incense in the air. Sai Fong brushed a pile of Chinese newspapers to the floor. "You sit, please," he said, motioning Mario to the chair he had cleared. "I back soon." And he disappeared through a door at the back of the shop.

Mario sat very quietly. He was afraid that if he moved, he would be buried under an avalanche of Chinese novelties. In a glass case right in front of him were a row of Chinese goddesses, carved in ivory. They all had the strangest smile on their lips—as if they knew something nobody else did. And they seemed to be staring straight at Mario. He tried to look at them, but he couldn't keep it up and had to look away.

In a few minutes Sai Fong came back into the room. He was carrying a cricket cage in the shape of a pagoda. There were seven tiers to it, each one a little smaller than the one below, and it ended in a slender spire. The lower parts of the cage were painted red and green, but the spire was golden. At one side was a gate with a tiny latch on it. Mario wanted to own the cage

46

so much that he tingled all over. But it looked awfully expensive.

Sai Fong held up the first finger of his right hand and said solemnly, "This velly ancient clicket cage. Once clicket who belonged to Empelor of all China lived in this cage. You know stoly of first clicket?"

"No, sir," said Mario.

"Velly good," said Sai Fong. "I tell." He set the cage down and took the clay pipe out of his pocket. When it was lit and a thread of smoke was curling up from the bowl, he used the pipe to emphasize what he said, drawing little designs, like Chinese writing, in the air.

"Long ago, in beginning of time, were no clickets. But was velly wise man, who knew all things. This man had name Hsi Shuai and spoke only tluth. All seclets were open to him. He knew thoughts of animals and men, he knew desire of flower and tlee, he knew destiny of sun and stars. Entire world was single page for him to read. And the high gods who lived in palace at summit of heaven loved Hsi Shuai because of tluth he spoke.

"Now flom many lands came men to hear their fate flom Hsi Shuai. To one he say, 'You velly good man. Live long as cedar tlee on mountain side.' To other he say, 'You wicked man—die soon. Good-bye.' But to all men Hsi Shuai speak only tluth. Of course wicked men most unhappy when hear what Hsi Shuai

48

say. They think, 'I wicked man—now evelyone know
how wicked I am.' So all together wicked men decide
to kill Hsi Shuai. Hsi Shuai know velly well they want
kill him—he know evelything—but he not care.
Within his heart, like smell of sweetness within lotus
blossom, Hsi Shuai have peace. And so he wait.

"But high gods, who live in palace at summit of
heaven, would not let Hsi Shuai be killed. More ple-
cious to them than kings was this one man who only
spoke tluth. So when wicked men laise swords above
Hsi Shuai, high gods change him into clicket. And man
who only spoke tluth and knew all things now sings
songs that no man undelstands and all men love. But
high gods undelstand, and smile. For to them beautiful
song of clicket is song of one who still speaks tluth
and knows all things."

Sai Fong stopped speaking and smoked his pipe
silently. Mario sat still too, looking at the cricket cage.
He was thinking about the story and how much he
wanted the cage. In his matchbox Chester Cricket had
listened carefully. He was very touched by the tale of
Hsi Shuai. Of course he couldn't tell if it was true, but
he sort of believed it, because he personally had always
thought that there was more to his song than just
chirping. As usual when he didn't know what else
to do, he rubbed one wing across the other. A single
clear note sounded in the shop.

The Cricket in Times Square

Sai Fong lifted his head. A smile curled up the ends of his ancient lips. "Ah so," he whispered. "Clicket has understood." He puffed a few more times.

Mario wanted to asked him how much the cage cost, but he was afraid to.

"Because this clicket so lemarkable," said Sai Fong, "I sell cage for fifteen cents."

Mario sighed with relief. He could afford that. In his pocket he found a nickel and a dime, all that was left of his weekly allowance, which was a quarter. "I'll take it, Mr. Fong," he said and handed Sai Fong the money.

"I also make plesent flee," said Sai Fong. He went behind the counter and took a little bell, no bigger than a honey bee, out of a drawer. With a piece of thread he hung it up inside the cage. Mario put Chester into the cage. The cricket jumped up and knocked against the bell. It tinkled faintly. "Sound like littlest bell in Silver Temple, far off up Yangtse River," said Sai Fong.

Mario thanked him for the bell and the story and everything. As he was about to leave the shop, Sai Fong said, "You want Chinee Fortune cookie?"

"I guess so," said Mario. "I never had one."

Sai Fong took down a can from the shelf. It was full of Fortune cookies—thin wafers that had been folded so there was an air space in each one. Mario bit into a cookie and found a piece of paper inside. He read what it said out loud: GOOD LUCK IS COMING YOUR WAY. BE READY.

"Eee hee hee!" laughed Sai Fong. "Velly good advice. You go now. Always be leady for happiness. Good-bye."

SEVEN

The Cricket Cage

That same night, after the Bellinis had gone home, Chester was telling Harry and Tucker about his trip to Chinatown. The cat and the mouse were sitting on the shelf outside, and Chester Cricket was crouched under the bell in the cage. Every minute or so, Tucker would get up and walk around to the other side of the pagoda. He was overcome with admiration for it.

"And Mr. Fong gave Mario a fortune cookie too," Chester was saying.

"I'm very fond of Chinese food myself," said Harry Cat. "I often browse through the garbage cans down in Chinatown."

Tucker Mouse stopped gaping at the cricket cage long enough to say, "Once I thought of living down there. But those Chinese make funny dishes. They make soup out of bird's nests and stew out of sharks' fins. They could make a soufflé out of a mouse. I decided to stay away."

A low rumble of a chuckle came from Harry Cat's

throat. "Listen to the mouse," he said and gave Tucker a pat on the back that sent him rolling over and over.

"Easy, Harry, easy," said Tucker, picking himself up. "You wouldn't know your own strength." He stood up on his hind legs and looked in through the red painted bars of the cage. "What a palace," he murmured. "Beautiful! You could feel like a king living in a place like this."

"Yes," said Chester, "but I'm not so keen on staying in a cage. I'm more used to tree stumps and holes in the ground. It makes me sort of nervous to be locked in here."

"Do you want to come out?" asked Harry. He sprung one of his nails out of the pad of his right forepaw and lifted the latch of the gate to the cage.

Chester pushed the gate and it swung open. He jumped out. "It's a relief to be free," he said, jumping around the shelf. "There's nothing like freedom."

"Say, Chester," said Tucker, "could I go in for a minute? I was never in a pagoda before."

"Go right ahead," said Chester.

Tucker scrambled through the gate into the cage and pranced all around inside it. He lay down, first on one side, then on the other, and then on his back. "If only I had a kimono now," he said, standing up on his hind legs again and resting one paw on a bar. "I feel like the Emperor of China. How do I look, Harry?"

"You look like a mouse in a trap," said Harry Cat.

"Every mouse should end up in a trap so nice," said Tucker.

"Do you want to sleep in the cage?" asked Chester.

"Oh—could I!" exclaimed the mouse. His idea of luxury was to spend a night in such surroundings.

"Sure," said Chester. "I prefer the matchbox anyway."

"There's only one thing," said Tucker, stamping with his left hind leg. "This floor. It's a little hard to sleep on."

"I'll go over and get a bunch of paper from the drain pipe," volunteered Harry Cat.

"No, it'll make a mess," said Tucker. "We don't want to get Chester in trouble with the Bellinis." He hesitated. "Um—maybe we could find something here."

"How about a piece of Kleenex," suggested Chester. "That's nice and soft."

"Kleenex would be good," said Tucker, "but I was wondering—" He paused again.

"Come on, Tucker," said Harry Cat. "You've got something on your mind. Let's have it."

"Well," Tucker began, "I sort of thought that if there were any dollar bills in the cash register—"

Harry burst out laughing. "You might know!" he said to Chester. "Who but this mouse would want to sleep on dollar bills?"

The Cricket Cage

Chester jumped into the cash register drawer, which was open as usual. "There's a few dollars in here," he called up.

"Plenty to make a mattress," said Tucker Mouse. "Pass some in, please."

Chester passed the first dollar bill up to Harry Cat, who took it over to the cage and reached it through the gate. Tucker took hold of one end of the bill and shook it out like a blanket. It was old and rumply.

"Careful you don't rip it," said Harry.

"I wouldn't rip it," said Tucker. "This is one mouse who knows the value of a dollar."

Harry brought over the second dollar. It was newer and stiffer than the first. "Let me see," said Tucker. He lifted a corner of each bill, one in either paw. "This new one can go on the bottom—I like a crispy, clean sheet—and I'll pull the old one over for a cover. Now, a pillow is what I need. Please look more in the cash register."

Harry and Chester searched the compartments of the open drawer. There was a little loose change, but not much else.

"How about a fifty cent piece?" said Harry.

"Too flat," answered Tucker Mouse.

The rear half of the drawer was still inside the cash register. Chester crawled back. It was dark and he couldn't see where he was going. He felt around until his head bumped against something. Whatever it was, it seemed to be big and round. Chester pushed and shoved and finally got it back out into the dim light of the newsstand. It was one of Mama Bellini's earrings, shaped like a sea shell, with sparkling little stones all over it.

"Would an earring do?" he shouted to Tucker.

"Well, I don't know," Tucker said.

"It looks as if it was covered with diamonds," said Harry Cat.

"Perfect!" called Tucker. "Send it along."

Harry lifted the earring into the cage. Tucker examined it carefully, like a jeweler. "I think these are fake diamonds," he said at last.

"Yes, but it's still very pretty," said Chester, who had jumped up beside them.

"I guess it'll do," said Tucker. He lay down on his side on the new dollar bill, rested his head on the earring and pulled the old dollar up over him. Chester and Harry heard him draw a deep breath of contentment. "I'm sleeping on money inside a palace," he said. "It's a dream come true."

Harry Cat purred his chuckle. "Good night, Chester," he said. "I'm going back to the drain pipe where I can stretch out." He jumped to the floor.

"Good night, Harry," Chester called.

Soft and silent as a shadow, Harry slipped out the opening in the side of the newsstand and glided over to the drain pipe. Chester hopped into his matchbox.

The Cricket in Times Square

He had gotten to like the feeling of the Kleenex. It was almost like the spongy wood of his old tree stump —and felt much more like home than the cricket cage. Now they each had their own place to sleep.

"Good night, Tucker," Chester said.

" 'Night, Chester," Tucker answered.

Chester Cricket burrowed down deeper into the Kleenex. He was beginning to enjoy life in New York. Just before he fell asleep, he heard Tucker Mouse sighing happily in the cage.

EIGHT

Tucker's Life Savings

Chester Cricket was having a dream. In his dream he was sitting on top of his stump back in Connecticut, eating a leaf from the willow tree. He would bite off a piece of leaf, chew it up and swallow it, but for some reason it didn't taste as good as usual. There was something dry and papery about it, and it had a bitter flavor. Still Chester kept eating, hoping that it would begin to taste better.

A storm came up in his dream. The wind blew clouds of dust across the meadow. They swirled around his stump, and Chester began to sneeze because the dust got in his nose. But he still held on to the leaf. And then he sneezed such a big sneeze that it woke him up.

Chester looked around him. He had been walking in his sleep and he was sitting on the edge of the cash register. The storm had been a gust of air that blew into the newsstand when the shuttle pulled up to the station. He was still choking from the dirt that flew around him. Chester looked down at his two front legs, half expecting to find the willow leaf. But it was no leaf he was holding. It was a two dollar bill and he had already eaten half of it.

He dropped the bill and leaped over to the cricket cage, where Tucker Mouse was sleeping peacefully. Chester shook the silver bell furiously; it rang like a fire alarm. Tucker jumped out from under his blanket of dollar bills and ran around the cage shouting. "Help! Fire! Murder! Police!"

Then he realized where he was and sat down panting. "What is the matter with you, Chester?' he said. "I could have died from fright."

"I just ate half of a two dollar bill," said Chester.

Tucker stared at him with disbelief. "You did *what*?" he asked.

"Yes," said Chester, "look." He fetched the ruined two dollar bill from the cash register. "I dreamed it was a leaf and I ate it."

"Oh oh oh oh," moaned Tucker Mouse. "Not a one dollar bill—not even a one dollar bill and a fifty cent piece—*two dollars* you had to eat! And from the Bellinis too—people who hardly make two dollars in two days."

"What am I going to do?" asked Chester.

"Pack your bags and go to California," said Tucker.

Chester shook his head. "I can't," he said. "They've been so good to me—I can't run away."

Tucker Mouse shrugged his shoulders. "Then stay and take the rap," he said. He crept out of the cage and examined the remains of the money. "There's still half of it left. Maybe we could put scotch tape along the edge and pass it off as a one dollar bill."

"No one would believe it," said Chester. He sat down, still forlornly holding the bill. "Oh dear—and things were going along so nicely."

Tucker Mouse put his bed clothes back in the cash register drawer and came to sit beside Chester. "Buck up," he said. "We could still figure something out, maybe."

They both concentrated for a minute. Then Tucker clapped his paws and squeaked, "I got it! Eat the rest of it and they'll never know what happened."

"They'd accuse each other of losing it," said Chester. "I don't want to make any bad feeling between them."

"Oh you're so honorable!" said Tucker. "It's disgusting."

"Besides, it tastes bad," added Chester.

"Then how about this," Tucker had a new idea. "We frame the janitor who cleans the station. I'll take the evidence over and plant it in his water closet. He whopped me with a mop last week. I would be glad to see him go to jail for a few days."

"No, no," said Chester. "We can't get somebody else in trouble."

"Then a stranger," said Tucker. "We tip over the

Kleenex, break the glass in the alarm clock and throw all the small change on the floor. They'll think a thief came in the night. You could even put a bandage on and make out like a hero. I could see it all—"

"*No!*" Chester interrupted him. "The damage we'd do would cost even more than the two dollars."

Tucker had one more idea: he was going to volunteer to go over and swipe two dollars from the lunch counter. But before he could suggest that, the top of the stand was suddenly lifted off. They had forgotten what time it was. Mama Bellini, who was on duty in the morning, stood towering, frowning down on them. Tucker let out a squeak of fear and jumped to the floor.

"Catch the mouse!" shouted Mama. She picked up a *Fortune* magazine—very big and heavy—and heaved it after Tucker. It hit him on the left hind leg just as he vanished into the drain pipe.

Chester Cricket sat frozen to the spot. He was caught red handed, holding the chewed up two dollars in his front legs. Muttering with rage, Mama Bellini picked him up by his antennae, tossed him into the cricket cage and locked the gate behind him. When she had put the newsstand in order, she pulled out her knitting and began to work furiously. But she was so angry she kept dropping stitches, and that made her angrier still.

Chester crouched in a far corner of the cage. Things

had been going so well between Mama and him—but that was all ruined now. He half expected that she would pick him up, cage and all, and throw him onto the shuttle tracks.

At eight-thirty Mario and Papa arrived. Mario wanted to go to Coney Island for a swim today, but before he could even say "Good morning," Mama Bellini stretched out her hand and pointed sternly at Chester. There he was, with the evidence beside him.

A three-cornered conversation began. Mama denounced Chester as a money eater and said further that she suspected him of inviting mice and other unsavory characters into the newsstand at night. Papa said he didn't think Chester had eaten the two dollars on purpose, and what difference did it make if a mouse or two came in? Mama said he had to go. Papa said he could stay, but he'd have to be kept in the cage. And Mario knew that Chester, like all people who were used to freedom, would rather die than live his life behind bars.

Finally it was decided that since the cricket was Mario's pet, the boy would have to replace the money. And when he had, Chester could come out again. Until then—the cage.

By working part time delivering groceries, when he wasn't taking care of the newsstand, Mario thought he could earn enough in a couple of weeks to get Chester out of jail. Of course that would mean no swimming at Coney Island, and no movies, and no nothing, but it was worth it. He fed the cricket his breakfast—left over asparagus tips and a piece of cabbage leaf. Chester had practically no appetite after what had happened. Then, when the cricket was finished, Mario said, "Good-bye," and told him not to worry, and went off to the grocery store to see about his job.

That night, after Papa had shut up the newsstand, Chester was hanging through the gilded bars of his cage. Earlier in the evening Mario had come back to feed him his supper, but then he had to leave right away to get in a few more hours of work. Most of the day Chester had spent inventing hopping games to try to keep himself entertained, but they didn't work, really. He was bored and lonely. The funny thing was that although he had been sleepy and kept wishing it were night, now that it was, he couldn't fall asleep.

Chester heard the soft padding of feet beneath him. Harry Cat sprang up and landed on the shelf. In a moment Tucker Mouse followed him from the stool, groaning with pain. He was still limping in his left hind leg where the *Fortune* magazine had hit him.

"How long is the sentence?" asked Harry.

"Until Mario can pay back the money," sighed Chester.

The Cricket in Times Square

"Couldn't you get out on bail for the time being?" asked Tucker.

"No," said Chester. "And anyway, nobody has any bail. I'm surprised they let me off that easily."

Harry Cat folded his front paws over each other and rested his head on them. "Let me get this straight," he said. "Does Mario have to work for the money as punishment—or does he just have to get it somewhere?"

"He just has to get it," said Chester. "Why should he be punished? I'm the one who ate the money."

Harry looked at Tucker—a long look, as if he expected the mouse to say something. Tucker began to fidget. "Say Chester, you want to escape?" he asked. "We can open the cage. You could come and live in the drain pipe."

"No," Chester shook his head. "It wouldn't be fair to Mario. I'll just have to serve out the time."

Harry looked at Tucker again and began tapping one of his paws. "Well?" he said finally.

Tucker moaned and massaged his sore spot. "Oh my poor leg! That Mama Bellini can sure heave a magazine. Feel the bump, Harry," he offered.

"I felt it already," said Harry. "Now enough of the stalling. You have money."

"Tucker has money?" said Chester Cricket.

Tucker looked nervously from one to the other. "I have my life's savings," he said in a pathetic voice.

68

Tucker's Life Savings

"He's the richest mouse in New York," said Harry. "Old Money Bags Mouse, he's known as."

"Now wait a minute, Harry," said Tucker. "Let's not make too much from a few nickels and dimes."

"How did you get money?" asked Chester.

Tucker Mouse cleared his throat and began wringing his two front feet. When he spoke, his voice was all choked up with emotion. "Years ago," he said, "when yet a little mouse I was, tender in age and lacking in experience, I moved from the sweet scenes of my childhood—Tenth Avenue, that is—into the Times Square subway station. And it was here that I learned the value of economicness—which means saving. Many and many an old mouse did I see, crawling away unwanted to a poor mouse's grave, because he had not saved. And I resolved that such a fate would never come to me."

"All of which means that you've got a pile of loot back there in the drain pipe," said Harry Cat.

"Just a minute, please, if you wouldn't mind," said Tucker. "I'll tell it in my own way." His voice became high and pitiful again. "So for all the long years of my youth, when I could have been gamboling—which means playing—with the other mousies, I saved. I saved paper, I saved food, I saved clothing—"

"Save time and get to the point," said Harry.

Tucker gave Harry a sour smile. "And I also saved money," he went on. "In the course of many years of scrounging, it was only natural I should find a certain amount of loose change. Often—oh, often, my friends," Tucker put his hand over his heart, "would I sit in the opening of my drain pipe, watching the human beings and waiting. And whenever one of them dropped a coin—*however small!*—pennies I love—I would dash out, at great peril to life and limb, and bring it back to my house. Ah, when I think of the tramping shoes and the dangerous galoshes—! Many times have I had my toes stepped on and my whiskers torn off because of these labors. But it was worth it! Oh, it was worth it, my friends, on account of now I have two half dollars, five quarters, two dimes, six nickels and eighteen pennies tucked away in the drain pipe!"

"Which makes two dollars and ninety-three cents," said Harry Cat, after doing some quick addition.

"And proud I am of it!" said Tucker Mouse.

"If you've got all that, why did you want to sleep on the two dollar bills in the cricket cage?" asked Chester.

"No folding money yet," said Tucker. "It was a new sensation."

"You can get Chester out and still have ninety-three cents left," said Harry Cat.

"But I'll be ruined," whimpered Tucker. "I'll be wiped out. Who will take care of me in my old age?"

"I will!" said Harry. "Now stop acting like a skin-flint and let's get the money."

Tucker's Life Savings

Chester rang the silver bell to get their attention. "I don't think Tucker should have to give up his life savings," he said. "It's his money and he can do what he wants with it."

Tucker Mouse poked Harry in the ribs. "Listen to the cricket," he said. "Acting noble and making me look like a bum. Of course I'll give the money! Wherever mice are spoken of, never let it be said that Tucker Mouse was stingy with his worldly goods. Besides, I could think of it as rent I pay for sleeping in the cage."

In order that Tucker could keep at least one of each kind of coin, Harry Cat figured out that they should bring over one half dollar, four quarters, one dime, five nickels and fifteen cents. That would leave the mouse with a half dollar, a quarter, a dime, a nickel and three cents.

"It's not a bad beginning," said Tucker. "I could make up the losses in a year, maybe."

The cat and the mouse had to make several trips back and forth between the drain pipe and the newsstand, carrying the money in their mouths. They passed the coins into the cage one by one, and Chester built them up into a column, starting with the half dollar on the bottom and ending with the dime, which was smallest, on top. It was morning by the time they were finished. They had just time enough to share half of a hot dog before Mama Bellini was due to open the stand.

Tucker's Life Savings

Mario came with her. He wanted to feed Chester early and then work all morning until he took over the newsstand at noon. When they lifted off the cover, Mama almost dropped her end. There was Chester, sitting on top of the column of change, chirping merrily.

Mama's first suspicion was that the cricket had sneaked out and smuggled all the money from the cash register into the cage. But when she looked in the drawer, the money from the night before was still there.

Mario had the idea that Papa might have left it as a surprise. Mama shook her head. She would certainly have known if he had two dollars to leave anybody.

They asked Paul, the conductor, if he'd seen anyone around the newsstand. He said no. The only thing he'd noticed was that that big cat who sometimes prowled through the station had seemed to be busier than usual last night. And of course they knew that he couldn't have had anything to do with replacing the money.

But whoever left it, Mama Bellini was good to her word. Chester was allowed out of the cage, and no further questions were asked. Although she wouldn't have admitted it for the world, Mama felt the same way about money that Tucker Mouse did. When you had it, you had it—and you didn't bother too much about where it came from.

73

NINE

The Chinese Dinner

Mario decided that there must be something wrong with Chester's diet if he was eating two dollar bills. He had been feeding him all the things he liked himself, but now it occurred to him that what was good for a boy might not be right for a cricket. So he made up his mind to take the matter to an expert.

Late one afternoon, when he got off duty at the newsstand, Mario cleaned up the cricket cage, gave Chester a dusting off with a Kleenex and took him to Chinatown to see Sai Fong. It was almost seven o'clock when he got there and the shop was closed. He peered through the window and could make out a crack of light under the door to the inner room. And he heard the choppy murmur of two voices talking together in Chinese.

Mario rapped on the glass. The voices stopped talking. He rapped again, louder. The inside door opened and Sai Fong came into the shop, squinting through the half light. When he saw Mario, his chin dropped

The Cricket in Times Square

and he said, "Ah!—is little clicket boy." He opened the door.

"Hello, Mr. Fong," said Mario. "I don't want to bother you, but I have a problem with my cricket."

"You come in, please," said Sai Fong, closing the door behind them. "Velly old fliend here—know evelything about clickets."

He led Mario into the next room, which was the kitchen. On a black, cast-iron stove there were half a dozen pots, steaming and singing. The table was laid with beautifully painted china plates. On them were pictures of Chinese ladies and gentlemen, dressed in colored gowns and robes, walking on little bridges over a calm, blue lake. Beside the places that had been set were two pairs of chopsticks, each one in its own paper wrapper.

A very old Chinese gentleman was sitting in a rocking chair next to the window. He had a thin gray beard that hung down from his chin, and was wearing a long red and gold robe that looked like the ones on the plates. When Mario came in, he stood up slowly, with his hands folded, and bowed. Mario had never had an old Chinese gentleman bow to him before and he didn't quite know what to do. But he thought he had better bow back. Then the Chinese man bowed again. And so did Mario.

They might have gone on bowing all night if Sai Fong hadn't said something in Chinese to his friend.

It sounded like this: "Che shih y hsi so ti erh tung," and it means, "This is the boy with the cricket." Mario and Chester stole a glance at each other, but neither one of them understood Chinese.

The old man, however, became very excited. He peered down through the bars of the cricket cage and exclaimed with delight. Then, drawing himself up to his full height, he made a very low and solemn bow. Chester bowed back and gave one of his most polite chirps. That pleased the Chinese gentleman very much. He and Sai Fong began laughing and talking together. It sounded like the cheerful clicking of hundreds of chopsticks.

When they were finished telling each other how fine a cricket Chester was, Sai Fong said to Mario, "You like Chinee food, please?"

"Yes, I do," answered Mario, "I guess." He had never had anything Chinese except chop suey, but he was awfully fond of that.

"You wait, please," said Sai Fong. He disappeared into the shop and came back in a minute with two new robes. "This for you," he said, helping Mario on with one. It was purple and lavender, and had designs of the sun, moon and stars stitched all over it. "And this mine," said Sai Fong, putting on his own robe, which was blue and green, covered with pictures of fish and reeds and water lilies.

The old Chinese gentleman whispered something to

The Chinese Dinner

Sai Fong, and Sai whispered an answer back in Chinese. "So solly," he said to Mario, "no robe small enough for clicket."

"Oh that's all right," said Mario.

"You sit, please," said Sai and brought another chair to the table.

Mario sat down and the Chinese gentleman sat opposite him. Sai Fong put the cricket cage in the middle of the table and then went back and forth to the stove, bringing over steaming bowls of Chinese food. Chester was very curious to see what it tasted like, since he had never even had chop suey.

"This chow yuk—Chinee vegetable," said Sai Fong, setting down the first bowl. There were all kinds of green vegetables in the chow yuk—string beans and pea pods, and also pieces of diced chicken. Next came the fried rice with pork, cooked a delicious brown, with a nutty, meaty flavor. Then chow mein with pan-fried noodles and cashew nuts. But it wasn't all soupy like the chow mein Mario had seen at the Automat. He could have made a meal just out of the pan-fried noodles alone. And last there was duck cooked with pineapples. The pieces of roasted duck were swimming in a luscious, sweet sauce. Finally Sai Fong brought over a big pot of something.

"You know what this is?" he asked and lifted the lid.

Mario looked in. "Tea," he said.

"Eee hee hee!" laughed Sai Fong. "You make velly

The Cricket in Times Square

good Chinaman," he said, and smiled broadly at Mario.

Mario had a hard time learning to use the chopsticks. They kept slipping out of his hand. "Make believe two velly long fingers," said Sai Fong.

"Two long fingers—two long fingers," Mario told himself over and over again. And then he could work them. He got so that he could almost feel the food on the end of them as he lifted it into his mouth.

Chester was served his dinner too. Sai Fong got a tiny saucer out of the cupboard and put a dab of each course on it for the cricket. And he had never tasted anything so good! He especially liked the chow yuk, because vegetables were his favorite. Every so often he would have to stop eating and chirp for joy. Whenever he did, the Chinese gentleman and Sai Fong smiled and chattered to each other in Chinese. Mario felt the same way Chester did, but he couldn't chirp. All he could do to show how much he was enjoying everything was to answer, "Yes, please," each time Sai Fong asked him if he wanted more.

When the four of them had eaten as much of the chow yuk and chow mein and pork fried rice and duck with pineapples as they wanted, Sai Fong brought out some candied kumquats for dessert. Mario had two and several more cups of tea. Chester was so full he could only nibble on a piece of one.

"Now," said Sai Fong, when they were all finished, "what is ploblem with clicket." He lit his white clay

80

The Chinese Dinner

pipe and the old Chinese gentleman lit one too. They sat smoking, with the wisps of smoke curling up around their chins, looking very wise, Mario thought.

"The problem is," Mario began, "that my cricket eats money." And he told them all about the two dollar bill. Sai Fong had to translate everything into Chinese for his friend. After each new sentence the old man would nod his head and say "ah" or "oh" or "mmm" in a serious voice.

"So I think he must not be getting the right things to eat," Mario concluded his story.

"Velly excellent deduction," said Sai Fong. He began talking rapidly in Chinese. Then he stood up and said, "You wait, please," and went into the shop. In a moment he was back, carrying a big book under his arm. As the two Chinese were reading it, they would stop now and then and mutter something to each other.

Mario went around behind them. Of course he couldn't read the Chinese characters, but there were pictures in the book too. One showed a princess sitting on an ivory throne. On a stand beside her was a cricket cage just like Chester's.

All of a sudden the Chinese gentleman began to squeak with excitement. "Yu le! Yu le!" he said, tapping the page with the stem of his pipe.

"Here is! Here is!" Sai Fong exclaimed to Mario. "This stoly of plincess of ancient China. Had clicket for pet and feed him mulbelly leaves. It say, 'Just as silk worm who eat of mulbelly tlee spin beautiful silk, so clicket who eat leaves spin beautiful song.' "

"Then we've got to find a mulberry tree," said Mario. The only one he knew of right off hand was in the Botanical Gardens in Brooklyn, and that had a fence around it.

"But I have tlee!" said Sai Fong, and his face curled up in a smile as wide as a Halloween pumpkin's. "Light outside window." He went to the window and pulled up the shade. In the courtyard outside a mulberry tree was growing. One of its branches almost stuck into the kitchen. Sai pulled off about a dozen leaves and put one in the cricket cage. But Chester didn't touch it.

Mario was dismayed. "He doesn't like it," he said.

"Oh he like!" said Sai Fong. "He just full of Chinee dinner now. Eee hee hee!"

And that was exactly the truth. Any other time Chester would have been gobbling up the leaf. But he was stuffed now. Just to show them that leaves were what he wanted, however, he managed to take one bite.

"You see?" said Sai Fong. "He eat leaf when he hungry."

Chester was feeling so contented that he had to sing for a while. Everyone listened very quietly. The only other sound was the creaking of the rocking chair,

The Chinese Dinner

which went very well with the cricket's song. Sai Fong and his friend were very touched by the concert. They sat with their eyes closed and expressions of complete peace on their faces. When it was over, the old Chinese gentleman blew his nose on a silk handkerchief he took out of his sleeve. His eyes were moist. Dabbing at them with the handkerchief, he whispered something to Sai Fong.

"He say it like being in palace garden to hear clicket sing," Sai Fong translated to Mario.

The boy thanked Sai Fong for the Chinese dinner, but said he would have to be going now, because it was late.

"You come back any time," said Sai Fong. He put the eleven mulberry leaves in a little box and gave it to Mario. "Plenty leaves on tlee. I save all for clicket."

Mario thanked him again. The old Chinese gentleman stood up and bowed. Mario bowed to him. Sai Fong bowed, and Mario bowed to him too. In the cage Chester was bowing to everybody. Mario backed towards the door, still bowing, and went out. It had been a very nice evening. He felt formal and polite from all the bowing, and he was glad that his cricket had been able to make the two Chinese gentlemen so happy.

TEN

The Dinner Party

Late one night Chester Cricket was very busy inside the newsstand. As soon as the Bellinis went home, he hopped out of the matchbox and began to clean up. First he pushed in the box so its sides were even and then slid it over beside the alarm clock. Next he pulled a piece of Kleenex out of the Kleenex box and dragged it back and forth across the shelf. When the shelf was dusted, he picked up the tissue paper in his two front legs and polished the cricket cage so its bars shone. He wiped off the glass in the front of the alarm clock and the radio too until he could see his own reflection. The dial of the clock was luminous and it shed a very soft green light. Chester wanted everything to be perfect on this particular evening. There was going to be a party.

It was exactly two months since Chester had arrived in New York, and the three animals wanted to celebrate the anniversary. Nothing too formal, you understand—just a little dinner for everyone. Tucker Mouse

The Dinner Party

had volunteered to let them use the drain pipe, but Chester didn't want to eat amidst all the waste paper and rubbish his friend had collected. So after many conferences, they resolved on the newsstand. It was sheltered, and quite big enough, and the radio could provide nice background music.

Tucker Mouse jumped up beside Chester. "How is the food coming, Tucker?" asked the cricket. Tucker had been put in charge of refreshments.

"Hic hic hic," laughed Tucker Mouse, rubbing his front feet together, "wait till I tell you." He lifted up one foot. "I have: two chunks liverwurst, one slice ham, three pieces bacon—from a bacon, lettuce and tomato sandwich—some lettuce and tomato—from said sandwich—whole-wheat, rye and white crusts, a big gob cole slaw, two squares from a Hershey chocolate bar, the end of an Oh Henry candy bar—*with* nuts!—and now comes the climax." Tucker paused. "*Iced* soft drinks!"

"How did you get the ice?" asked Chester.

"Wait, I'll tell you," said Tucker, "All day I've been hiding by the lunch counter. When the soda jerks made a coke I grabbed the ice they spilled, which I then took to the drain pipe. There," he went on with especial pride, "it is happening I have a heat-proof, insulated bag saved up for just such an occasion. I put in the ice, shut up the opening—we have ice! Nice, eh?"

The Cricket in Times Square

He sat back on his haunches and grinned at Chester.

"Very nice," said Chester. "Where have you got the drinks?"

"In paper cups," said Tucker. "And no mixing of drinks either. For each kind soft drink—another cup."

"That's wonderful," said the cricket with admiration.

"Oh it's nothing really," said Tucker, waving a foot. "I mean, its something—but nothing too much." He looked around at the shelf and clock and everything. "You are to be congratulated on the cleanliness. Of course it isn't as important as food-getting, but to be clean is very nice too."

While they were talking, Harry Cat came in through the opening at the side of the newsstand. Chester hopped down, like a good host, to greet his new guest.

"How was the concert?" he asked. Harry had been down to Washington Square to hear an open air concert of chamber music. How you could play chamber music outdoors Chester didn't understand—but it was New York and anything could happen.

"Very good," answered Harry. "But I don't think the violinist played nearly as well as you do."

It made Chester very happy to hear that, but he had to turn away so Harry wouldn't see him blush.

"Harry, help me with the food," said Tucker. He jumped down to the floor and scurried over to the drain pipe.

The Dinner Party

The mouse and the cat put all the different courses over to one side with the soft drinks so everyone could just go up and help himself. It was buffet style. Tucker and Chester sat on the shelf and Harry, who was taller, sat on the stool. But his head was on a level with theirs.

Tucker Mouse took great pride in cooling the soft drinks. There were four cups, one with Coca Cola, one with Pepsi, one root beer, and the last orange pop. Tucker put a big piece of ice in each and then made a show of stirring them up with a straw he had found that afternoon.

"Ah," he sighed. "Where but New York could a mouse have ice in his Coca Cola?"

"We should have music," said Harry. He reached over and flicked on the radio.

First they got a news report. But that wouldn't do for a party. Harry twisted the dial and went through a quiz show, an amateur hour, and a play about the deep South before he got what he wanted. Music is very nice for a party because it gives you time to eat your fill without having to make conversation.

Harry Cat was working on his second piece of Oh Henry candy bar when he suddenly stopped munching and listened to the tune the radio was playing. His head began to sway from side to side.

"That's my favorite song," he said, beginning to hum along with it.

"Sing it, Harry," said Chester Cricket.

The Cricket in Times Square

"You don't know what you're letting yourself in for," blurted out Tucker Mouse through a mouthful of bacon, lettuce and tomato sandwich.

But Harry was in a party mood, so he cleared his throat and began:

"When I'm calling youuuuuuuu

Oooo-oooo-oooo

Oooo-oooo-oooo—"

Harry had a delightful yowl that went very well with the lyrics of the song.

"You see what I told you?" groaned Tucker.

Harry went right on, however:

"Will you answer truuuuuu

Oooo-oooo-oooo

Oooo-oooo-oooo?"

"Maybe we should turn back to the amateur hour," said Tucker Mouse, helping himself to the Hershey bar.

"I think Harry sings beautifully," said Chester.

"You sing now, Chester," said Harry Cat.

Secretly the cricket was very anxious to perform for them, but he had to have some encouragement first. He limbered his wings and said, "It's not really singing, you know—"

"Singing, playing—who cares, as long as it doesn't sound like Harry," said Tucker Mouse. He slurped up the last of the orange soda and they all fell silent.

It was well along in August by now, and just the

time of the year that crickets all over the world like most. Chester hadn't done nearly as much chirping as usual this summer because he was living in New York, but tonight he played to his heart's content. He thought of his meadow and the stump, the brook and the old willow tree. The song swelled up from his wings and filled the newsstand.

When it was over, Tucker and Harry applauded and congratulated Chester. "Now play us something we know," suggested Harry Cat.

"Well I don't know if I can," said Chester. "All my songs are my own compositions."

"Listen to the radio and play what it does," said Harry. He turned up the music.

Chester cocked his head on one side. The radio was playing the "Blue Danube Waltz." When he had heard enough to memorize the melody, Chester joined in. And he played it perfectly! The cricket was such a natural musician that he not only chirped the tune—in a few minutes he was making up variations and spinning them out without ever losing the rhythm of the waltz. He found that by tilting his wings he could make the notes go higher or lower, just as he wanted.

Chester got an ovation from his friends. Harry Cat, who had crept into the Metropolitan Opera House a few times and knew how people acted there, shouted, "Bravo, Chester! Bravo!" Of course after such a sample of his talent for imitating songs, his friends insisted that he keep on. And Chester was happy to oblige.

The Dinner Party

There's nothing like a good audience to encourage a performer.

The next selection from the radio was a group of Italian folk songs. Chester picked out the different melodies and chirped them along with the orchestra. After the folk songs came a group of operatic arias. It was easier for Chester to play the ones written for tenors than the ones for sopranos, contralto and basses, but he did them all beautifully.

Each time he stopped after singing a new piece, the animals shouted, "More! More! More!" So Chester went right on. Now came a South American rhumba. The rhythm was very tricky and it took the cricket a few minutes to catch on to it, but once he had it, he never lost the beat. Chirping away, he sounded like a pair of lively castanets.

"Imagine!" exclaimed Tucker Mouse, "he plays pop as well as classical."

Tucker was feeling very lively himself because of all the soda water he had swallowed. The South American tempo began to excite him. He jumped up and started to dance around the shelf.

Harry Cat burst out laughing, but that didn't bother Tucker. He was a carefree soul. "Chester can play—I can dance," he panted. "We should go into vaudeville."

"If you danced as well as he played, you could," said Harry.

"So I'm just learning," said Tucker and threw himself into a wild twirl next to Papa Bellini's pipe.

He couldn't see where he was going and he toppled over into the box of kitchen matches. The box flipped over. A shower of matches fell around the shelf and onto the cement floor. There were several yellow bursts and the sharp scratch that a match makes when it's lit. Most of them fell far enough away from the wooden walls so they could burn themselves out without danger. But one match, unluckily, struck right next to a pile of that morning's newspapers. The spurt of flames it sent up lit the frayed edge of the papers and quickly spread over the whole bundle.

"Watch out!" shouted Chester. Harry Cat leaped up to the shelf just in time to keep his tail from being burned. The cricket was the first to realize what had happened—and what was likely to happen if they didn't put the fire out. "Get the Coca Cola," he said. "Pour it over."

"I drank it all," shouted Tucker.

"You would!" said Chester. "Is there any ice?"

Harry and Tucker dumped what was left in the insulated bag down on the flames. But it wasn't enough. The fire sputtered, died down and then flared up again, larger than ever.

"Maybe we can smother it," said Harry.

There was a pile of magazines on the very edge of the shelf, just above the fire. Harry strained and pushed and succeeded in toppling them over. They all peered over the edge to see if the fire was out.

The Cricket in Times Square

"Oh fine!" said Tucker. "She's still burning and you blocked the hole to get out!"

They were trapped. Harry and Tucker jumped down and started pulling away the magazines furiously. But the fire crept closer and they had to back away.

"What a way to go," said Tucker. "I should have stayed on Tenth Avenue."

For a moment Chester got panicky. But he forced his thoughts back into order and took stock of the situation. And an idea struck him. In one leap he jumped onto the alarm clock, landing right on the button that set off the alarm. The old clock began ringing so wildly it shook itself around the shelf in a mad dance. Chester hopped back to his friends.

"Any alarm in a fire," he said.

They waited, crouched against the wall. On the opposite side of the stand the flames were lapping against the wood. Already the paint on it had begun to blister.

Chester could hear voices outside the newsstand. Even at this hour there were always a few people in the station. Somebody said, "What's that?"

"I smell smoke," said another. Chester recognized the voice. It was Paul, the conductor on the shuttle. There was a sound of footsteps running away, then running back again, and a hammering began. The newsstand shook all over.

94

The Dinner Party

"Somebody get the other side," said Paul.

The cover was wrenched off. Clouds of smoke billowed up. The people standing around were astonished to see, through the fumes and glare of the fire, a cat, a mouse, and a cricket, running, jumping, to safety.

ELEVEN

The Jinx

From the drain pipe the animals watched Paul put out the fire. He dragged what papers he could out of the newsstand and got a bucket of water to douse the rest. And he watered down the walls to make sure they wouldn't flare up later. When the danger was over, he called up Papa Bellini on the telephone.

"What a mess," said Tucker Mouse, looking at the soggy, smouldering piles of papers and magazines.

No one knew what to say.

"What are you going to do, Chester?" said Harry Cat finally.

"I'm going back there," said Chester. "If the Bellinis find me gone, they'll think I set the fire and ran."

"What makes you think they won't think you set the fire and stayed?" said Tucker.

"I'll have to take that chance," said Chester. Before the cat or the mouse could say anything to stop him, he hopped over to the newsstand.

Paul had told the engineer that he would miss a few

trips on the shuttle and was waiting for the Bellinis. He didn't want anyone monkeying with the cash register while the cover was off. The conductor thought that the cups and bags from the animals' party had been left by Mario or Papa. While he was taking them over to a trash barrel, Chester jumped up on the shelf. Nothing there had been burned, but there was a smokey smell to everything. The cricket took a down-hearted leap into the cage and settled himself for whatever might come.

It didn't take the Bellinis long to arrive. They had taken a taxi. And when the Bellinis took a taxi, you can be sure it was an emergency. Chester could hear them hurrying down the steps from the street. Papa was trying to soothe Mama, who was wheezing heavily from asthma and excitement. When she saw the heaps of scorched magazines and newspapers, she began to moan and shake her head. Papa eased her down onto the stool, but it was still covered with water and she stood up again with a wet spot on her skirt.

"Ruin—we're ruined," she sobbed. "Everything's burned."

Papa comforted her as best he could by saying that it was only a few stacks of the *Ladies' Home Journal* that had been lost. But Mama wouldn't believe that anything less than complete destruction had come to them all.

Mario, who brought up the rear of this sad parade,

The Jinx

thought first for the safety of his cricket. He saw that Chester was in his cage, though, and decided that it would be best to keep quiet until Mama's outburst of grief had subsided.

Paul told them what had happened: how he smelled smoke and heard the alarm clock ringing. Then he came to the part about the animals who had escaped from the burning newsstand.

"*So*—!" said Mama Bellini, all her despair changing into anger. "Animals in the newsstand again! Didn't I tell you?" She lifted her forefinger at Mario. "Didn't I say the cricketer would ask in his pals? He probably set the fire. He's a firebug!"

Mario didn't have a chance to speak. He would open his mouth to defend Chester, but before he could say a thing, the words were drowned in Mama's flood of reproaches. She had found someone on whom she could blame her unhappiness and there was no stopping her.

When a pause came, Mario said meekly, "My cricket would never do anything like burn up our newsstand."

"The fact remains," said Mama, "we had a fire!"

"But crickets are good luck—" Mario began.

"Good luck!" said Mama indignantly. "He eats money—he commits arson! He's a jinx, that's what. He's good luck going backwards. And he's got to go." She folded her arms across her chest. It was an attitude that Mario knew meant the absolute end of everything.

99

The Cricket in Times Square

"I could keep him somewhere else," the boy offered.

"No," said Mama, shaking her head as firmly as a door being closed. "He's a jinx. He goes."

Papa put his finger to his lips as a signal that Mario shouldn't say anything more and the two of them began to clean up. They carted away all the hopelessly burned magazines and tried to salvage some that had only been scorched. Mario mopped the floor of the newsstand while Mama spread out papers to dry. By the time they were finished, it was almost the hour for the first wave of commuters.

Chester was lying on the floor of the cricket cage. He felt guilty, because even if he hadn't set it, in a way the fire was his fault. If he hadn't invited everyone into the newsstand, it wouldn't have happened. And it was his playing of the rhumba that had made Tucker want to dance, and so tip over the matches. And he did eat the two dollar bill. He began to believe that he really was a jinx.

During the early morning rush hour Mario was especially eager in his shouts of "Paper, mister," and "*Time* or *Life*, mister." Papa was more active than usual too. But Mama sat glumly on the stool with a gray, determined look on her face. Despite the fact that the selling that morning went very well, she wouldn't change her mind. After the rush was over, Papa went out to buy a new lock.

Chester heard a soft scratching from behind the

The Jinx

Kleenex box. A familiar face peeked out. "What's going on?" whispered Tucker Mouse.

"Are you crazy?" said Chester, under his breath. "All they need is to catch you here."

"I had to find out how you were doing," said Tucker.

"They're going to throw me out," sighed Chester.

"Oh oh oh," Tucker moaned. "And it was me that did it. Supposing I give you the rest of my life's savings. Maybe we could buy them off."

Chester leaned his black little head up against the bars of the cricket cage. "Not this time," he said. "Mama's got her mind made up. I don't blame her either. I wish I'd never come to New York."

"Oh Chester," wailed Tucker Mouse, "don't say that! You'll make me feel like a rat. And I'm only a mouse."

"It's not your fault, Tucker," said Chester. "But I've been nothing but bad luck to them since I came."

Without knowing what he was doing, the cricket began to chirp to ease his feelings. He found that it helped somehow if you sang your sadness. He wasn't paying much attention and just by accident he played the first few notes of an Italian folksong he had heard the night before. It was so melancholy, and yet so sweet, that it fitted his mood exactly.

Mama Bellini was untying a bundle of *Herald Tribune*s when she heard the chirping. At first she didn't know what it was. "Che cos' e questa?" she said in Italian, which means, "What's that?"

Chester stopped playing.

"Chi cantava?" said Mama. "Who was singing?"

Mario looked at his mother. Usually when she spoke in Italian it meant that she was in a good mood. But that couldn't be true today.

Now Tucker Mouse was a very good judge of character—both animal and human. He thought he heard a kind of softness in Mama Bellini's voice. "Play some more," he whispered to Chester.

"She hates me," said Chester. "It'll only make her more angry."

"Do like I tell you!' commanded the mouse urgently.

So Chester started to chirp again. He was in such disgrace anyway, what difference could it make? The piece he was playing was called "Come Back to Sorrento," and by the greatest good luck, it happened to be Mama Bellini's favorite song. Back in Naples, Italy, when Papa was courting her before they came to America, he used to come beneath her window on a moonlit night and sing this ballad to the plunking of an old guitar. As the cricket chirped, the whole scene came back to Mama: the still, warm night, the moon shining down on the velvety Bay of Naples, and Papa singing to her. Tears welled up in her eyes as she thought of the by-gone times, and very softly she began to murmur the words to the song.

The Cricket in Times Square

Chester Cricket had never played with so much skill before. When he heard Mama singing, he slowed his tempo so she could keep up without straining. When she was loud, he was too—and then softer when she got choked up with emotion and her voice dwindled. But always his chirping carried her along, keeping her on the right beat and the right tune. He was the perfect accompanist.

Mario was dumbfounded. He stared astonished at the cricket cage and then at his mother. It was just as marvelous for his mother to be singing as it was for a cricket to chirp familiar songs. Sometimes, when she was very happy, Mama Bellini whistled, and once or twice Mario had heard her hum. But now here she was crying and warbling like an Italian nightingale!

Chester finished "Come Back to Sorrento."

"Keep it up! Keep it up!" squeaked Tucker Mouse. "She's a sucker for sad songs."

Before Mama's mood had a chance to wear off, Chester began chirping the selections from opera that he had played during the party. Mama didn't know the words to the operas, but she hummed some of the tunes along with him. Mario was as still as stone.

Papa Bellini came back from the locksmith's. Coming down the stairs he was surprised not to hear his wife and Mario calling out the newspapers. But when he got nearer the newsstand, he was even more sur-

The Jinx

prised to hear the strains of the Grand March from
Aïda coming from the cricket cage.

"He chirps *opera?!*" exclaimed Papa. His eyes looked
as big and startled as two hard boiled eggs.

"Shhh," said Mama with a wave of her hand.

Chester's memory for music was perfect. He only
had to hear a piece once to remember it forever. When
he had finished all the operatic numbers, he stopped.
"Should I go on with the pop tunes?" he whispered
to Tucker Mouse, who was still hidden behind the
Kleenex box.

"Wait a while," said Tucker. "See what happens."

Mama Bellini had a dreamy look in her eyes. She put
her arm around her son and said, "Mario, no cricketer
who sings 'Torn a Sorrento' so beautifully could possibly start a fire. He could stay a while longer."

Mario threw his arms around his mother's neck.

"You hear? You hear?" squealed Tucker Mouse.
"You can stay! Oh boy oh boy oh boy! And this is
only the beginning. I'll be your manager—okay?"

"Okay," said Chester.

And so began the most remarkable week in Chester
Cricket's—or any cricket's—life.

TWELVE

Mr. Smedley

It was two o'clock in the morning. Chester Cricket's new manager, Tucker Mouse, was pacing up and down in front of the cricket cage. Harry Cat was lying on the shelf with his tail drooping over the edge, and Chester himself was relaxing in the matchbox.

"I have been giving the new situation my serious consideration," said Tucker Mouse solemnly. "As a matter of fact, I couldn't think of anything else all day. The first thing to understand is: Chester Cricket is a very talented person."

"Hear! hear!" said Harry. Chester smiled at him. He was really an awfully nice person, Harry Cat was.

"The second thing is: talent is something rare and beautiful and precious, and it must not be allowed to go to waste." Tucker cleared his throat. "And the third thing is: there might be—who could tell?—a little money in it, maybe."

"I knew that was at the bottom of it," said Harry.

"Now wait, please, Harry, please, just listen a

minute before you begin calling me a greedy rodent," said Tucker. He sat down beside Chester and Harry. "The newsstand is doing lousy business—right? *Right!* If the Bellinis were happy, Mama Bellini wouldn't be always wanting to get rid of him—right? *Right!* She likes him today because he played her favorite songs, but who could tell how she might like him tomorrow?"

"And also I'd like to help them because they've been so good to me," put in Chester Cricket.

"But naturally!" said Tucker. "And if a little bit of the rewards of success should find its way into a drain pipe where lives an old and trusted friend of Chester—well, who is the worse for that?"

"I still don't see how we can make any money," said Chester.

"I haven't worked out the details," said Tucker. "But this I can tell you: New York is a place where the people are willing to pay for talent. So what's clear is, Chester has got to learn more music. I personally prefer his own compositions—no offense, Chester."

"Oh no," said the cricket. "I do myself."

"But the human beings," Tucker went on, "being what human beings are—and who could blame them? —would rather hear pieces written by themselves."

"But how am I going to learn new songs?" asked Chester.

"Easy as pie," said Tucker Mouse. He darted over to the radio, leaned all his weight on one of the dials and snapped it on.

"Not too loud," said Harry Cat. "The people outside will get suspicious."

Tucker twisted the dial until a steady, soft stream of music was coming out. "Just play it by ear," he said to Chester.

That was the beginning of Chester's formal musical education. On the night of the party he had just been playing for fun, but now he seriously set out to learn some human music. Before the night was over he had memorized three movements from different symphonies, half a dozen songs from musical comedies, the solo part for a violin concerto, and four hymns— which he picked up from a late religious service.

The next morning, which was the last Sunday in August, all three Bellinis came to open the newsstand. They could hardly believe what had happened yesterday and were anxious to see if Chester would continue to sing familiar songs. Mario gave the cricket his usual breakfast of mulberry leaves and water, which Chester took his time eating. He could see that everyone was very nervous and he sort of enjoyed making them wait. When breakfast was over, he had a good stretch and limbered his wings.

Since it was Sunday, Chester thought it would be nice to start with a hymn, so he chose to open his concert with "Rock of Ages." At the sound of the first notes, the faces of Mama and Papa and Mario broke into smiles. They looked at each other and their eyes told how happy they were, but they didn't dare to speak a word.

During the pause after Chester had finished "Rock of Ages," Mr. Smedley came up to the newsstand to buy his monthly copy of *Musical America*. His umbrella, neatly folded, was hanging over his arm as usual.

"Hey, Mr. Smedley—my cricket plays hymns!" Mario blurted out even before the music teacher had a chance to say good morning.

"And opera!" said Papa.

"And Italian songs!" said Mama.

"Well, well, well," said Mr. Smedley, who didn't believe a word, of course. "I see we've all become very fond of our cricket. But aren't we letting our imagination run away with us a bit?"

"Oh no," said Mario. "Just listen. He'll do it again."

Chester took a sip of water and was ready to play some more. This time, however, instead of "Rock of Ages," he launched into a stirring performance of "Onward Christian Soldiers."

Mr. Smedley's eyes popped. His mouth hung open and the color drained from his face.

"Do you want to sit down, Mr. Smedley?" asked Papa. "You look a little pale."

"I think perhaps I'd better," said Mr. Smedley, wiping his forehead with a silk handkerchief. "It's rather a shock, you know." He came inside the newsstand and sat on the stool so his face was just a few inches away from the cricket cage. Chester chirped the second verse of "Onward Christian Soldiers," and finished with a soaring "Amen."

"Why the organist played that in church this morning," exclaimed the music teacher breathlessly, "and it didn't sound *half* as good! Of course the cricket isn't as loud as an organ—but what he lacks in volume, he makes up for in sweetness."

"That was nothing," said Papa Bellini proudly. "You should hear him play *Aïda*."

"May I try an experiment?" asked Mr. Smedley.

All the Bellinis said "yes" at once. The music teacher whistled the scale—do, re, mi, fa, sol, la, te, do. Chester flexed his legs, and as quickly as you could run your fingers up the strings of a harp, he had played the whole scale.

Mr. Smedley took off his glasses. His eyes were moist. "He has absolute pitch," he said in a shaky voice. "I have met only one other person who did. She was a soprano named Arabella Hefflefinger."

Chester started to play again. He went through the two other hymns he'd learned—"The Rosary" and "A Mighty Fortress is Our God"—and then did the violin concerto. Naturally, he couldn't play it just as it was written without a whole orchestra to back him

up, but he was magnificent, all things considered.

Once Mr. Smedley got used to the idea that he was listening to a concert given by a cricket, he enjoyed the performance very much. He had special praise for Chesters "phrasing," by which he meant the neat way the cricket played all the notes of a passage without letting them slide together. And sometimes, when he had been deeply moved by a section, the music teacher would touch his chest over his heart and say, "That cricket has it *here!*"

As Chester chirped his way through the program, a crowd collected around the newsstand. After each new piece, the people applauded and congratulated the Bellinis on their remarkable cricket. Mama and Papa were fit to burst with pride. Mario very happy too, but of course he had thought all summer that Chester was a very unusual person.

When the playing was over, Mr. Smedley stood up and shook hands with Papa, Mama and Mario. "I want to thank you for the most delightful hour I have ever spent," he said. "The whole world should know of this cricket." A light suddenly spread over his face. "Why I believe I shall write a letter to the musical editor of the New York *Times*," he said. "They'd certainly be interested."

And this is the letter Mr. Smedley wrote:

To the Music Editor of the New York *Times* and to the People of New York—

Mr. Smedley

Rejoice, oh New Yorkers—for a musical miracle has come to pass in our city! This very day, Sunday, August 28th, surely a day which will go down in musical history, it was my pleasure and privilege to be present at the most beautiful recital ever heard in a lifetime devoted to the sublime art. (Music, that is.) Being a musicologist myself, and having graduated—with honors—from a well-known local school of music, I feel I am qualified to judge such matters, and I say, without hesitation, that never have such strains been heard in New York before!

"But who was the artist?" the eager music lover will ask. "Was it perchance some new singer, just lately arrived from a triumphant tour of the capitals of Europe?"

No, music lovers, it was not!

"Then was it some violinist, who pressed his cheek with love against his darling violin as he played?"

Wrong again, music lovers.

"Could it have been a pianist—with sensitive, long fingers that drew magic sounds from the shining ivory keys?"

Ah—music lovers, you will never guess. It was a cricket! A simple cricket, no longer than half my little finger—which is rather long because I play the piano—but a cricket that is able to chirp operatic, symphonic and popular music. Am I wrong then in describing such an event as a miracle?

And where is this extraordinary performer? Not in Carnegie Hall, music lovers—nor in the Metropolitan Opera House. You will find him in the

The Cricket in Times Square

newsstand run by the Bellini family in the subway station at Times Square. I urge—I implore!—every man, woman and child who has music in his soul not to miss one of his illustrious—nay, his *glorious*—concerts!

enchantedly yours,
Horatio P. Smedley

P.S. I also give piano lessons. For information write to: H. P. Smedley
1578 West 63rd Street
New York, N. Y.

THIRTEEN

Fame

The music editor of the New York *Times* was quite surprised to get Mr. Smedley's letter, but he believed in the freedom of the press and had it printed on the theatrical and musical page of the paper. The next morning, thousands of people—at home, over the breakfast table and on buses and trains coming into New York—read about Chester.

The Bellinis got to the newsstand very early. Papa opened the *Times* bundle and thumbed through a copy looking for the letter. When he found it, he read it aloud to Mama and Mario. Then he folded the paper and put it back on the stack to be sold.

"So," said Papa. "We have a celebrity in our midst."

The celebrity was just at that moment having himself a big yawn in the cricket cage. He had been up most of the night with his manager and Harry Cat, learning new pieces. After eating breakfast and having another stretch, he tested his wings against each other, like a violinist making sure that his violin was in tune. The wings were fine. This time of year they almost itched to chirp. Chester ran over the scales a few times and started to play.

His first selection was something he had heard the night before called "A Little Night Music." It was by a man named Mozart. Chester and Tucker and Harry had all been delighted by "A Little Night Music." They thought it was a very good piece for the cricket to learn because they had heard it first at night, and also because Chester was quite a little person himself. It was lovely music too, with little tunes that sounded like insects hopping around and having a grand time.

As Chester played, the station began to fill up with the usual commuters. People collected around the newsstand—some drawn by the chirping, and others because they wanted to see the cricket they'd read about. And as always in New York, when a little crowd formed, more people came just to see what the others were looking at. Bees do that, and so do human beings.

Somebody asked who was playing.

"A cricket," a man answered.

"Oh stop joking!" the first man said and burst out laughing.

In front of him a little lady with a feather in her hat, who was enjoying the music, turned around and whispered "shhhh!" very angrily.

The Cricket in Times Square

In another part of the station a man was reading Mr. Smedley's letter, and two other men were also reading it over his shoulders.

"My gosh!" said the one on the right, "A cricket. Who would have believed it?"

"It's a fake," said the man on the left. "Probably a record."

The man in the middle, who owned the paper, snapped it shut. "It *isn't* a fake!" he said. "It's a little living creature—and it sings beautifully! I'm going to give up my season ticket at the Philharmonic."

Everywhere people were talking and arguing and listening to Chester.

Mario made a pile of old magazines and put the cricket cage on top of them so everyone could see better and hear more clearly. When Chester finished one number, a shout of "More! More!' rang through the station. The cricket would catch his breath, have a sip of water, flex his wings and begin a new selection as fast as he could.

And the crowd grew and grew. Mama Bellini had never seen such a crowd around the newsstand. But she wasn't one to be so dazed by good fortune that she missed out on such a chance. Taking a bundle of *Times* under one arm, she worked her way around, murmuring softly—so as not to disturb the music lovers—"Read about the cricket, read about the cricket, it's in the New York *Times*."

People snapped up the papers like candy. Mama had

TRACK-1

to keep going back to the newsstand for new loads. And in less than half an hour the whole stock of the *Times* had been sold.

"Don't sit with your eyes shut," Mama whispered to Papa. (Papa Bellini was one of those people who enjoy listening to music most with their eyes closed.) She put a bunch of *Musical America* into his arms. "Try these—it's a good time now."

Papa sighed, but did as she asked him. And in a little while all the copies of *Musical America* were gone too. It is safe to say that there had never been such an an interest in music in the Times Square subway station as there was on that morning.

Over in the drain pipe Tucker Mouse and Harry Cat were listening too—Harry with his eyes closed like Papa Bellini. There were so many human beings that they couldn't even see the newsstand. But they could hear Chester chirping away, on the other side of all the heads and legs and backs. His clear notes filled the station.

"Didn't I tell you?" said Tucker between pieces. "Look at them all. There's a fortune in this. I wish one of us was big enough to pass the hat."

But Harry only smiled. He was happy right where he was, just sitting, enjoying the music.

And the crowd kept on growing. That first day alone, there were seven hundred and eighty-three people late to work because they had stopped to listen to Chester.

Fame

During the next few days, other papers besides the *Times* began to run articles on the cricket. Even *Musical America* sent an editor (an assistant editor) down to hear a recital. And Chester was news on the radio and television. All the announcers were talking about the remarkable insect who was delighting throngs in the Times Square subway station.

The Bellinis decided that the best times for Chester to play were early in the morning and late in the afternoon, since that was when the station was fullest. Concerts began at eight A.M. and four-thirty P.M. and usually lasted an hour and a half—not including encores.

Business boomed at the newsstand. Mama made sure that extra loads of magazines and newspapers were delivered. But even so, by closing time they had sold out completely. Mama Bellini, by the way, turned out to be the best friend a cricket ever had. At noon she would rush home and fix Chester some delicacy for lunch, like a midget fruit salad or an entire vegetable dinner so small¹ you could serve it on a silver dollar. Chester really preferred his mulberry leaves, but he ate everything so as not to hurt her feelings.

Sai Fong, who had seen Chester's picture in the paper, kept Mario supplied with leaves. He and the Chinese gentleman dug out two collapsible chairs from his attic and came uptown every day at eight and four-thirty to hear Chester's new programs.

Mr. Smedley was there at least once a day too. He brought a tape recorder and made recordings of all the new pieces Chester learned. And during the intermissions—there was always an intermission of ten minutes half way through the concert—he delivered short talks on musical appreciation to the audiences.

So by Thursday Chester Cricket was the most famous musician in New York City. But now here is a strange thing: he wasn't really happy—not the way he used to be. Life didn't seem to have the fun and freedom it had had before.

For one thing, although he thought that glory was very nice, Chester found that it made you tired. Two concerts a day, every day, was an exhausting program. And he wasn't used to playing on schedule. Back home in the meadow, if the sun felt nice, or the moon was full, or if he wanted to have a musical conversation with his friend the lark, he would chirp because the mood was on him. But here he had to begin performing at eight and four-thirty whether he felt like it or not. Of course he was very glad to be helping the Bellinis, but a lot of the joy was gone from his playing.

And there was something else: Chester didn't like being looked at. It wasn't so bad while he was playing. Everyone was quiet, enjoying the music. But after the performance was over, the human beings crowded around and put their faces down close to the bars and poked their fingers through. Souvenir hunters had

taken his paper cup and even the pieces of mulberry leaves that were left over. Chester knew they didn't mean any harm—but he couldn't get used to the idea that millions of eyes were staring at him. It got so bad that when the concerts were over, he took to crawling into the matchbox and pushing up a piece of Kleenex to block the entrance.

Then, on Thursday, three things happened that upset him very much. The first was September. It was the first day of a new month. Chester happened to glance up at the top of a copy of the *Times,* where the date was, and there he saw it: SEPTEMBER 1— a new month, and a new season too. Autumn was almost upon them. For some reason the thought of September, with all its changes, made Chester feel very small and lost.

And that evening, while he was playing, a brown leaf, the first leaf of the fall, blew into the station and landed right next to the cricket cage. Now this leaf had come from New Jersey. A playful gust of wind danced it over the Hudson River, and up Forty-second Street, and whisked it down the subway entrance. Chester was in the middle of a song when the leaf came down. It was such a shock to see this little reminder of all that was happening in the country that for a moment he couldn't continue. But then he realized where he was and forced himself to go on. Mario was the only one who noticed the break in the playing.

But the worst thing happened after the concert was over. Chester was leaning up against the matchbox when suddenly two fingers began to work their way through the bars of the cage towards the little silver bell. It wasn't Mama's fingers, or Papa's, or Mario's— Chester knew the hands of the Bellinis. Somebody was trying to steal the bell! The cricket chirped an alarm just as the man was about to pull it down.

Papa turned around, saw what was happening and shouted, "Hey! What are you doing?" The man disappeared in the crowd.

Mama and Mario had been outside selling off the last of the day's papers. They came running back to the newsstand. "What is it?" panted Mama.

"A thief," said Papa.

"Is my cricket all right?" asked Mario anxiously.

"Yes," said Papa. "He's in the matchbox."

Mario picked up the box and looked in. There was Chester, piling a Kleenex against the opening. "You can come out now," the boy said. "It's safe," but Chester wouldn't come out. Mario had noticed that the cricket took to hiding after each recital, and it worried him.

Mama Bellini was convinced that the man was a kidnapper—or rather, cricketnapper—not just a thief. But Papa told them how he had been going straight for the bell.

"That bell belongs to my cricket," said Mario. "Mr.

Fong gave it to him." He unfastened the bell and put it way back in the cash register drawer, next to Mama's earring, so it wouldn't tempt anyone else.

Chester was still hiding in the matchbox. Mario gently pulled the Kleenex away and whispered, "Please come out." Chester stirred and chirped, but stayed where he was.

"What's the matter with him?" said Papa.

"I think he may be sick," said Mario. He coaxed Chester with a mulberry leaf. The cricket poked his head out of the matchbox. When he saw that the crowd had broken up, he jumped into the palm of Mario's hand.

"You should take him to a bug doctor," said Mama. "What do you call them?"

"Entomologists," said Mario, holding the leaf for Chester to nibble.

"Take him to an entololomist," said Mama.

"He might just be tired," said Papa. "We could give him a rest for a few days."

Chester had eaten as much of the leaf as he wanted. He gave a short chirp for "thank you" and jumped back in the box.

"He isn't happy any more," said Mario.

"How do you know?" said Mama.

"I can tell," said Mario. "I know how I'd feel if I was a cricket." Mario put the matchbox in the cricket cage. "Next week school begins," he said. "You've got to promise you'll take good care of him while I'm not here."

"We will, Mario," said Papa. "We like him too, you know."

The boy stood looking down at the cage. His forehead was drawn together in a worried frown. "I almost wish he hadn't come to New York—if he isn't going to be happy here," he said finally.

Chester heard him and thought about what he said. He thought about it while the Bellinis were fitting on the cover. And later, in the darkness, after they'd gone home, he was still thinking about it. Then, quickly, like a lock snapping into place, something was decided in his mind. Chester felt very relieved after the decision had been made. He sighed, and his wings and his legs all relaxed as he waited there for Tucker Mouse.

FOURTEEN

Orpheus

Chester didn't have long to wait. In a few minutes Tucker came bounding into the newsstand and up to the stool and the shelf. Harry followed him, ambling silently along, as always.

Tucker Mouse took himself very seriously now that he was the manager of a famous concert artist. "Good evening, Chester," he said. "You should excuse the suggestion, please, but I thought your tempo was off tonight in the 'Stars and Stripes Forever.' You couldn't afford to relax just because you're on top, you know. And now, let us begin the practicing."

Chester crawled out of the matchbox. "Can't I even say hello to Harry?" he asked.

"So say hello!" said Tucker Mouse. "Hello, Harry— Hello, Chester. So, the greetings being over, let us get on with the practicing."

Chester looked at Harry and shook his head. The cat smiled and winked.

Tucker twisted the dial. Wearily Chester crossed

The Cricket in Times Square

his wings into the position for playing. There was an Irish jig on the radio. The cricket prepared to fling himself into the first wild strains of the jig, but suddenly he dropped his wings and said, "I'm just not up to it tonight."

"What's the matter?" asked Tucker.

"I don't feel like playing," said Chester.

"You don't feel like playing!" the mouse exclaimed. "That's like the sun saying, 'I don't feel like shining.'"

"Well, sometimes there are cloudy days," said the cricket. "Can't I have a rest too?"

"Um um um—" Tucker Mouse was very much flustered.

"Let him take a day off," said Harry Cat. "What's the matter, Chester? Is fame beginning to get you down?"

"I guess I'm just feeling Septemberish," sighed Chester. "It's getting towards autumn now. And it's so pretty up in Connecticut. All the trees change color. The days get very clear—with a little smoke on the horizon from burning leaves. Pumpkins begin to come out."

"We can go up to Central Park," said Tucker. "The trees change their color there too."

"It isn't the same," said Chester. "I need to see a shock of corn." He paused and fidgeted nervously. "I didn't mean to tell you yet, but you may as well know. I'm going to—I'm going to retire."

"Retire!" shrieked Tucker Mouse.

"Yes, retire," said Chester softly. "I love New York, and I love to have all those people listen to me, but I love Connecticut more. And I'm going home."

"But—but—but—" Tucker Mouse was spluttering helplessly.

"I'm sorry, Tucker, but I've made up my mind," said Chester.

"What about Mario?" said the mouse.

"He wants me to be happy," Chester answered. "He said he wished I'd never come to New York if I was going to be miserable."

"But all the human beings!" Tucker waved his front legs. "All the suffering thousands your playing gives pleasure to—what about them?"

"My playing gives pleasure to a lot of people in Connecticut too," said Chester.

"Who?" asked Tucker Mouse scornfully.

"Oh—woodchucks and pheasants and ducks and rabbits, and everybody else who lives in the meadow or the brook. I had a bullfrog tell me once that he enjoyed my music more than anything else—except the sound of rain on the pond where he lived. And another time a fox was chasing a rabbit around my stump, and they both stopped to listen while I was playing."

"What happened?" said Tucker.

"The rabbit made it to his hole," said Chester. "I

began the fox's favorite song just as he was about to chase him again, and he stayed to listen. Now I couldn't do that for any human being in the subway station."

"I wouldn't be so sure," said Tucker Mouse. He turned to the cat. "Harry, say something! Make him stay!"

"Yes, Harry," said Chester. "What's your opinion?"

Harry Cat sat perfectly still a moment. His whiskers were wiggling, which was a sign that he was thinking very hard.

"My opinion," he said finally, "is that it's Chester's life and he should do what he wants. What good is it to be famous if it only makes you unhappy? Other people have retired at the peak of their careers. In all honesty, however, I must add that I will be dreadfully sorry to see him go."

Tucker Mouse scratched his left ear—always a good sign. Something about that phrase—"peak of their careers"—struck his imagination. "There would be a lot of glory, I suppose," he said. "Giving everything up—just when he's on top. What a *gesture*!" The idea took hold of his tiny mouse's mind. "I can see it all now. At the summit of his success—that's the same as the peak of his career, isn't it?"

"Just the same," said Harry Cat, grinning at Chester.

"At the summit of his success—he vanishes!" Tucker raced back and forth on the shelf. "The papers will go crazy! Where is he? Where did he go? Nobody knows.

He leaves behind only a beautiful memory. How touching! How lovely!" His voice cracked.

"The only thing that worries me," said Chester Cricket, "is what will happen to the newsstand if I go."

"Don't worry about that," said Harry Cat. "This newsstand has been touched by the Golden Finger of Fortune! They'll probably make a national park out of it."

"Do you really think so?" said Chester.

"Well, even if they don't," Harry answered, "I'm sure the Bellinis will do very well. They're famous now too."

"So when do you plan to make it final?" asked Tucker.

Chester thought a moment. "Today is Thursday," he said. "How about tomorrow night?"

"Friday is an excellent day for retiring," said the mouse. "If I ever retire from scrounging, it will be on a Friday."

Chester Cricket heaved a big sigh. "Oh—I feel better," he said. "If you want me to learn some new pieces for tomorrow now, I will."

"Why bother?" said Harry Cat. "Tonight's your last full night in New York. You may as well enjoy yourself."

"Come to the drain pipe!" said Tucker Mouse. "We'll have a party in honor of your retirement. I have plenty of food—and no matches to burn the place up!"

So the three friends hopped, scuttled and padded across to Tucker's home, where a fine, farewell feast was held. And it was thoroughly enjoyed by all.

The next day, at five minutes to six, Chester was about to begin the last public piece he would ever play in New York City. It was Friday night, the busiest time of all. Besides the commuters coming home from work, the station was swarming with men and women who were leaving the city for the weekend, on their way to Grand Central Station. But they all stopped to listen to Chester. There were so many people crowded around the newsstand that the police had to keep aisles to and from the subway trains open with ropes.

The cricket had just finished his most beautiful concert. For this final encore he wanted to play the sextet from an opera called *Lucia di Lammermoor*. It had been written for six people, but even though he was very talented, Chester could only do one part. So he took the tenor's music because it carried the main theme most of the time.

They didn't know it, but Chester was playing the sextet in honor of the whole Bellini family. It was Papa's favorite of favorites, and Mario and Mama loved it too. Chester wanted them always to remember him playing this piece. As he struck up the first notes, a sigh of pleasure came from Papa Bellini and he settled

back on the stool with his eyes closed. Mama leaned against the side of the newsstand, resting her head on one hand. At the sound of the familiar strains, without her meaning to, a smile spread over her face. Mario was bending over the cricket cage, fascinated by the way Chester moved his wings when he played. And he was awfully proud that it was his pet that everyone was listening to.

Over in the drain pipe opening, Tucker and Harry were sitting side by side. The animals were the only ones who knew that it was his farewell performance, and it made them feel solemn and a little sad. But the music was so sweet that they couldn't help but be happy too.

"It's the sextet from *Loochy the Murmurer*," announced Tucker Mouse, who had become quite an expert on all things musical during the past week.

"Too bad there aren't five other crickets like Chester," whispered Harry Cat. "They could do the whole thing."

Then they too were silent, and for as long as the music lasted, no one moved a hair or a whisker.

Chester's playing filled the station. Like ripples around a stone dropped into still water, the circles of silence spread out from the newsstand. And as the people listened, a change came over their faces. Eyes that looked worried grew soft and peaceful; tongues left off chattering; and ears full of the city's rustling were rested by the cricket's melody.

The men at the other newsstands heard Chester and stopped shouting for people to buy their newspapers and magazines. Mickey the counterman heard him and left off making a Coca Cola. The three girls came to the door of the Loft's candy store. Passengers coming up from the lower level paused before asking the policemen for directions. No one dared break the hush that had taken hold of the station.

Above the cricket cage, through a grate in the sidewalk, the chirping rose up to the street. A man who was walking down Broadway stopped and listened. Then someone else did. In a minute a knot of people was staring at the grate.

"What is it?"

"An accident?"

"What's happening?"

Whispers passed back and forth in the crowd. But as soon as there was a moment of silence, everyone could hear the music.

People overflowed the sidewalk into the street. A policeman had to stop traffic so nobody would get hurt. And then everyone in the stopped cars heard Chester too. You wouldn't think a cricket's tiny chirp could carry so far, but when all is silence, the piercing notes can be heard for miles.

Traffic came to a standstill. The buses, the cars, men and women walking—everything stopped. And what was strangest of all, no one minded. Just this once, in the very heart of the busiest of cities, everyone was perfectly content not to move and hardly to breathe. And for those few minutes, while the song lasted, Times Square was as still as a meadow at evening, with the sun streaming in on the people there and the wind moving among them as if they were only tall blades of grass.

FIFTEEN

Grand Central Station

After the concert Mama and Papa Bellini had to go off for the evening. They left Mario in charge of the newsstand and told him they would be back later to help him close up. The boy took Chester out of the cricket cage, balancing him on one finger. He was glad that they were going to have some time to themselves, for a change.

First he took a cardboard sign he had printed saying "NEXT CONCERT 8 A.M." and leaned it up against the cage. "That'll keep people from bothering us about when you play next," he said. Chester chirped. But he knew he wouldn't be playing the next morning at 8 A.M.

"Now we have supper," said Mario. He unwrapped a fried egg sandwich for himself and brought over a mulberry leaf from the cash register drawer for Chester. (The mulberry leaves were kept in the compartment next to the quarters.) For dessert there was a Hershey bar—a smidgin from one corner for Chester and the rest for Mario.

141

Then, after dinner, they began to play games. Leap-frog was one they enjoyed very much. Mario made a fist and Chester had to jump over it. The trick was that Mario could put his fist anywhere he wanted inside the newsstand, and Chester still had to land just on the other side of it. They kept score for half an hour. Chester had thirty-four hits to five misses—which was quite good, considering the hard places Mario found to put his fist.

Hide and seek was fun too. Mario closed his eyes and counted, and Chester hid somewhere in the news-stand. Since there were piles of papers all over, and since he was very small himself, the cricket found lots of good hiding places. If Mario couldn't find him in a few minutes, Chester would give a quick chirp as a hint. But it was hard to tell whether the sound came from behind the alarm clock, or in the Kleenex box, or from the cash register drawer. If Chester had to chirp three times, it was understood he had won the game.

About ten o'clock Mario began to yawn and they stopped playing. The boy sat on the stool, with his back resting on the side of the stand, and Chester gave him a private recital. He didn't play any of the things he'd learned—just made up one of his own pieces as he went along. And he played very softly so the people in the station wouldn't hear and come over. He wanted this to be for Mario alone. As he listened, the boy's

eyes slowly closed and his head dropped over on one shoulder. But through his sleep he could still hear the cricket's silvery chirping.

Chester ended his song and sat on the shelf, looking at Mario. A "psst" sound came up from the floor—just as it had on his first night in the newsstand. The cricket looked over. There was Tucker again, gazing up at him. It struck Chester what a funny, but likable expression the mouse's face always wore.

"You better hurry," whispered Tucker. "Harry found a timetable and the train leaves in an hour."

"I'll be over in a minute," Chester called down to him.

"Okay," the mouse answered and scooted across the station floor.

Mario's right hand was cupped in his lap. The cricket jumped down into the palm of it. In his sleep the boy felt something and stirred. Chester was afraid he would wake him up, but Mario only settled in a new position. The cricket lifted his wings and drew them lightly together. There was all of his love, and good-bye too, in that one chirp. Mario smiled at the familiar sound.

Chester looked around at the newsstand—the box of Kleenex, the alarm clock, Papa's pipe. When he came to the cash register, he paused. Quickly springing to the edge of the drawer, he vanished back into the darkness. When he came out again, the little silver

bell was hooked over his left front leg. Holding it tight against him to muffle the tinkle, he jumped to the stool, to the floor and out the crack.

"What's the bell for?" asked Tucker when he arrived at the drain pipe.

"It's mine," said Chester. "Mario said so. And I want it to remember everything by."

Tucker Mouse rummaged through the crowded corner of his home which was the pantry and found a tiny package bound with scotch tape. "I packed some supper for you to have on the train," he said. "Nothing very much—I mean, delicious, of course—a piece of steak sandwich and a chocolate cooky—but none too good for such talent!"

"Thank you, Tucker," said Chester. He wanted to sound very cheerful, but the words came out sort of gulpy.

"Well, I guess we should go," said Harry Cat.

"I guess so," said Chester. He took one more look through the drain pipe. From down the tracks came the murmur of the shuttle. Mario was still asleep in the newsstand. The neon lights shed their endless blue-green glow. The cricket wanted to remember every detail. "It's funny," he said at last. "Sometimes the subway station looks almost beautiful."

"I've always thought so," said Tucker.

"Come on," said Harry Cat. He and Tucker padded

along beside Chester up to the sidewalk.

Above ground the night was fresh and clear—not as hot as summer nor as cool as autumn. Chester jumped up on Harry's back and took hold of the fur there. He could probably have made it down to Grand Central Station jumping by himself, but it saved time to be given a ride. And crossing the streets would have been a problem too for a cricket raised in Connecticut. But Tucker and Harry were experts at traveling in the city. Not a single human being saw them as they glided soundlessly under the cars that lined Forty-second Street.

When they reached the station, Harry led the way through a maze of pipes and deserted rooms and back halls down to the level where the trains were. He was a great explorer, Harry Cat, and knew most of the secret ins and outs of New York City.

The Late Local Express was leaving on track eighteen. Chester hopped onto the rear platform of the last car and settled himself in a corner that would be out of the wind. And there were only a few minutes left before the train started.

"How will you know when you get to Connecticut?" said Tucker. "You were buried under sandwiches when you left there."

"Oh I'll know!" said Chester. "I'll smell the trees and I'll feel the air, and I'll know."

No one said anything. This was the hardest time of all.

"Maybe you could come back for a visit next summer," said Harry Cat. "Now that you know the way."

"A return engagement at the newsstand," said Tucker.

"Maybe I can," said Chester.

There was another pause. Then the train gave a lurch forward. And as soon as it started to move, the three friends all found that they still had millions of things to say. Harry shouted that Chester should take care of himself—Tucker told him not to worry about the Bellinis, he would look after them—and Chester just kept chirping good-bye as long as he could.

For a while the two who stayed could see the cricket waving, but then the train rushed away into the darkness of the tunnel and was lost. They strained their eyes through the blackness.

"Did you hear another chirp?" said Tucker after a minute.

"Come on, Tucker," said Harry. "Let's go home."

Together they tramped up to Times Square and down the drain. Neither one of them said a word. They looked out the hole. Mario hadn't waked up yet.

"He's going to be very unhappy," said Tucker.

Mama and Papa Bellini came up the stairs from the lower level, Mama gasping from the climb. Papa gently shook Mario awake. Suddenly Mama's gasping stopped and she said, "Where's the cricketer?"

They searched the newsstand completely but couldn't find him. Mama was sure that the man who tried to steal the bell had come back and kidnapped him. She wanted to call the police. Papa thought he might have stepped out for a breath of fresh air. But Mario was quiet, thinking. He looked through the cash register drawer, in every compartment, and then pulled the drawer out completely. The back space was empty—except for Mama's earring.

"He won't come back," said Mario.

"How do you know?" said Papa.

"The bell's gone," said Mario. "You and I and the cricket were the only ones who knew where it was. If a thief had taken it, he would have taken the money from the cash register too. My cricket took it and went home." Mario's voice dropped off abruptly. But then it came back firm. "And I'm glad."

Mama was about to exclaim that she didn't believe it, but Papa put his hand on her arm. He said he wasn't sure—but it might be. Mario didn't say anything more, because he *knew*. They put on the cover to the newsstand and went down to their subway.

Tucker Mouse looked at Harry Cat. "He knows," he said.

Harry swished his tail around him and said, "Yes, he knows."

They were so relieved that for a minute neither of

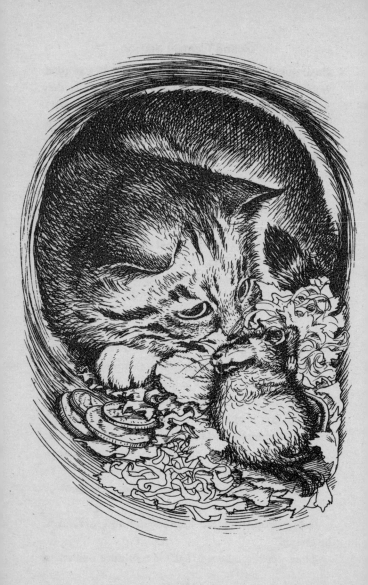

them moved. It was all right now. Chester was gone, but it was all right for everybody. After a while they went back and lay down on the shredded newspapers. But neither of them seemed to be able to fall asleep.

Tucker Mouse changed his position. "Harry," he said.

"Yes?" said Harry Cat.

"Maybe next summer we could go to the country."

"Maybe we can."

"I mean—the country in Connecticut," said Tucker.

"I know what you mean," said Harry Cat.

Turn the page for a special preview
of the
1996 NEWBERY HONOR BOOK

(ISBN 0-385-32175-9)

Enter the hilarious world of ten-year-old Kenny and his
family, the Weird Watsons of Flint, Michigan. There's
Momma, Dad, little sister Joetta, Kenny, and Byron, who's
thirteen and an "official juvenile delinquent." When Momma
and Dad decide it's time for a visit to Grandma, Dad comes
home with the amazing Ultra-Glide, and the Watsons set out
on a trip like no other. They're heading south. They're going
to Birmingham, Alabama, toward one of the darkest
moments in American history.

**Don't miss *The Watsons Go to Birmingham–1963*
by Christopher Paul Curtis.
On sale now from Delacorte Press!**

1. And You Wonder Why We Get
Called the Weird Watsons

It was one of those super-duper-cold Saturdays. One of those days that when you breathed out your breath kind of hung frozen in the air like a hunk of smoke and you could walk along and look exactly like a train blowing out big, fat, white puffs of smoke.

It was so cold that if you were stupid enough to go outside your eyes would automatically blink a thousand times all by themselves, probably so the juice inside of them wouldn't freeze up. It was so cold that if you spit, the slob would be an ice cube before it hit the ground. It was about a zillion degrees below zero.

It was even cold inside our house. We put sweaters and hats and scarves and three pairs of socks on and still were cold. The thermostat was turned all the way up and the furnace was banging and sounding like it was about to blow up but it still felt like Jack Frost had moved in with us.

All of my family sat real close together on the couch under a blanket. Dad said this would generate a little heat but he didn't have to tell us this, it seemed like the cold automatically made us want to get together and huddle up. My little sister, Joetta, sat in the middle and all you could see were her eyes because she had a scarf wrapped around her head. I was next to her, and on the outside was my mother.

Momma was the only one who wasn't born in Flint so the cold was coldest to her. All you could see were her eyes too, and they were shooting bad looks at Dad. She always blamed him for bringing her all the way from Alabama to Michigan, a state she called a giant icebox. Dad was bundled up on the other side of Joey, trying to look at anything but Momma. Next to Dad, sitting with a little space between them, was my older brother, Byron.

Byron had just turned thirteen so he was officially a teenage juvenile delinquent and didn't think it was "cool" to touch anybody or let anyone touch him, even if it meant he froze to death. Byron had tucked the blanket between him and Dad down into the cushion of the couch to make sure he couldn't be touched.

Dad turned on the TV to try to make us forget how cold we were but all that did was get him in trouble. There was a special news report on Channel 12 telling about how bad the weather was and Dad groaned when the guy said, "If you think it's cold now, wait until tonight, the temperature is expected to drop into record-low territory, possibly reaching the negative twenties! In fact, we won't be seeing anything above zero for the next four to five days!" He was smiling when he said this but none of the Watson family thought it was funny. We all looked over at Dad. He just shook his head and pulled the blanket over his eyes.

Then the guy on TV said, "Here's a little something we can use to brighten our spirits and give us some hope for the future: The temperature in Atlanta, Georgia, is forecast to reach . . ." Dad coughed real loud and jumped off the couch to turn the TV off but we all heard the weatherman say, ". . . the mid-seventies!" The guy might as well have tied Dad to a tree and said, "Ready, aim, fire!"

"Atlanta!" Momma said. "That's a hundred and fifty miles from home!"

"Wilona . . . ," Dad said.

"I knew it," Momma said. "I knew I should have listened to Moses Henderson!"

"Who?" I asked.

Dad said, "Oh Lord, not that sorry story. You've got to let me tell about what happened with him."

Momma said, "There's not a whole lot to tell, just a story about a young girl who made a bad choice. But if you do tell it, make sure you get all the facts right."

We all huddled as close as we could get because we knew Dad was going to try to make us forget about being cold by cutting up. Me and Joey started smiling right away, and Byron tried to look cool and bored.

"Kids," Dad said, "I almost wasn't your father. You guys came real close to having a clown for a daddy named Hambone Henderson. . . ."

"Daniel Watson, you stop right there. You're the one

who started that 'Hambone' nonsense. Before you started that everyone called him his Christian name, Moses. And he was a respectable boy too, he wasn't a clown at all."

"But the name stuck, didn't it? Hambone Henderson. Me and your granddaddy called him that because the boy had a head shaped just like a hambone, had more knots and bumps on his head than a dinosaur. So as you guys sit here giving me these dirty looks because it's a little chilly outside ask yourselves if you'd rather be a little cool or go through life being known as the Hambonettes."

Me and Joey cracked up, Byron kind of chuckled and Momma put her hand over her mouth. She did this whenever she was going to give a smile because she had a great big gap between her front teeth. If Momma thought something was funny, first you'd see her trying to keep her lips together to hide the gap, then, if the smile got to be too strong, you'd see the gap for a hot second before Momma's hand would come up to cover it, then she'd crack up too.

Laughing only encouraged Dad to cut up more, so when he saw the whole family thinking he was funny he really started putting on a show.

He stood in front of the TV. "Yup, Hambone Henderson proposed to your mother around the same time I did. Fought dirty too, told your momma a pack of lies about me and when she didn't believe them he told her a pack of lies about Flint."

Dad started talking Southern-style, imitating this

Hambone guy. "Wilona, I heard tell about the weather up that far north in Flint, Mitch-again, heard it's colder than inside a icebox. Seen a movie about it, think it was made in Flint. Movie called *Nanook of the North*. Yup, do believe for sure it was made in Flint. Uh-huh, Flint, Mitch-again.

"Folks there live in these things called igloos. According to what I seen in this here movie most the folks in Flint is Chinese. Don't believe I seen nan one colored person in the whole dang city. You a 'Bama gal, don't believe you'd be too happy living in no igloo. Ain't got nothing against 'em, but don't believe you'd be too happy living 'mongst a whole slew of Chinese folks. Don't believe you'd like the food. Only thing them Chinese folks in that movie et was whales and seals. Don't believe you'd like no whale meat. Don't taste a lick like chicken. Don't taste like pork at all."

Momma pulled her hand away from her mouth. "Daniel Watson, you are one lying man! Only thing you said that was true was that being in Flint is like living in a igloo. I knew I should have listened to Moses. Maybe these babies mighta been born with lumpy heads but at least they'da had *warm* lumpy heads!

"You know Birmingham is a good place, and I don't mean just the weather either. The life is slower, the people are friendlier—"

"Oh yeah," Dad interrupted, "they're a laugh a minute down there. Let's see, where was that 'Coloreds Only' bathroom downtown?"

"Daniel, you know what I mean, things aren't perfect

but people are more honest about the way they feel"—she took her mean eyes off Dad and put them on Byron—"and folks there do know how to respect their parents."

Byron rolled his eyes like he didn't care. All he did was tuck the blanket farther into the couch's cushion.

Dad didn't like the direction the conversation was going so he called the landlord for the hundredth time. The phone was still busy.

"That snake in the grass has got his phone off the hook. Well, it's going to be too cold to stay here tonight, let me call Cydney. She just had that new furnace put in, maybe we can spend the night there." Aunt Cydney was kind of mean but her house was always warm so we kept our fingers crossed that she was home.

Everyone, even Byron, cheered when Dad got Aunt Cydney and she told us to hurry over before we froze to death.

Dad went out to try and get the Brown Bomber started. That was what we called our car. It was a 1948 Plymouth that was dull brown and real big, Byron said it was turd brown. Uncle Bud gave it to Dad when it was thirteen years old and we'd had it for two years. Me and Dad took real good care of it but some of the time it didn't like to start up in the winter.

After five minutes Dad came back in huffing and puffing and slapping his arms across his chest.

"Well, it was touch and go for a while, but the Great Brown One pulled through again!" Everyone cheered, but me and Byron quit cheering and started frowning right away. By the way Dad smiled at us we knew what was coming next. Dad pulled two ice scrapers out of his pocket and said, "O.K., boys, let's get out there and knock those windows out."

We moaned and groaned and put some more coats on and went outside to scrape the car's windows. I could tell by the way he was pouting that Byron was going to try and get out of doing his share of the work.

"I'm not going to do your part, Byron, you'd better do it and I'm not playing either."

"Shut up, punk."

I went over to the Brown Bomber's passenger side and started hacking away at the scab of ice that was all over the windows. I finished Momma's window and took a break. Scraping ice off of windows when it's that cold can kill you!

I didn't hear any sound coming from the other side of the car so I yelled out, "I'm serious, Byron, I'm not doing that side too, and I'm only going to do half the windshield, I don't care what you do to me." The windshield on the Bomber wasn't like the new 1963 cars, it had a big bar running down the middle of it, dividing it in half.

"Shut your stupid mouth, I got something more important to do right now."

I peeked around the back of the car to see what By was up to. The only thing he'd scraped off was the outside mirror and he was bending down to look at himself in it. He saw me and said, "You know what, square? I must be adopted, there just ain't no way two folks as ugly as your momma and daddy coulda give birth to someone as sharp as me!"

He was running his hands over his head like he was brushing his hair.

I said, "Forget you," and went back over to the other side of the car to finish the back window. I had half of the ice off when I had to stop again and catch my breath. I heard Byron mumble my name.

I said, "You think I'm stupid? It's not going to work this time." He mumbled my name again. It sounded like his mouth was full of something. I knew this was a trick, I knew this was going to be How to Survive a Blizzard, Part Two.

How to Survive a Blizzard, Part One had been last night when I was outside playing in the snow and Byron and his running buddy, Buphead, came walking by. Buphead has officially been a juvenile delinquent even longer than Byron.

"Say, kid," By had said, "you wanna learn somethin' that might save your stupid life one day?"

I should have known better, but I was bored and I think maybe the cold weather was making my brain slow, so I said, "What's that?"

"We gonna teach you how to survive a blizzard."

"How?"

Byron put his hands in front of his face and said, "This is the most important thing to remember, O.K.?"

"Why?"

"Well, first we gotta show you what it feels like to be trapped in a blizzard. You ready?" He whispered something to Buphead and they both laughed.

"I'm ready."

I should have known that the only reason Buphead and By would want to play with me was to do something mean.

"O.K.," By said, "first thing you gotta worry about is high winds."

Byron and Buphead each grabbed one of my arms and one of my legs and swung me between them going, "*Wooo,* blizzard warnings! Blizzard warnings! *Wooo!* Take cover!"

Buphead counted to three and on the third swing they let me go in the air. I landed headfirst in a snowbank.

But that was O.K. because I had on three coats, two sweaters, a T-shirt, three pairs of pants and four socks along with a scarf, a hat and a hood. These guys couldn't have hurt me if they'd thrown me off the Empire State Building!

After I climbed out of the snowbank they started laughing and so did I.

"Cool, Baby Bruh," By said, "you passed that part of the test with a B-plus, what you think, Buphead?"

Buphead said, "Yeah, I'd give the little punk a A."

They whispered some more and started laughing again.

"O.K.," By said, "second thing you gotta learn is how to keep your balance in a high wind. You gotta be good at this so you don't get blowed into no polar bear dens."

They put me in between them and started making me spin round and round, it seemed like they spun me for about half an hour. When slob started flying out of my mouth they let me stop and I wobbled around for a while before they pushed me back in the same snowbank.

When everything stopped going in circles I got up and we all laughed again.

They whispered some more and then By said, "What you think, Buphead? He kept his balance a good long time, I'm gonna give him a A-minus."

"I ain't as hard a grader as you, I'ma give the little punk a double A-minus."

"O.K., Kenny, now the last part of Surviving a Blizzard, you ready?"

"Yup!"

"You passed the wind test and did real good on the balance test but now we gotta see if you ready to graduate. You remember what we told you was the most important part about survivin'?"

"Yup!"

"O.K., here we go. Buphead, tell him 'bout the final exam."

Buphead turned me around to look at him, putting my back to Byron. "O.K., square," he started, "I wanna make sure you ready for this one, you done so good so far I wanna make sure you don't blow it at graduation time. You think you ready?"

I nodded, getting ready to be thrown in the snowbank real hard this time. I made up my mind I wasn't going to cry or anything, I made up my mind that no matter how hard they threw me in that snow I was going to get up laughing.

"O.K.," Buphead said, "everything's cool, you 'member what your brother said about puttin' your hands up?"

"Like this?" I covered my face with my gloves.

"Yeah, that's it!" Buphead looked over my shoulder at Byron and then said, "*Wooo!* High winds, blowing snow! *Wooo!* Look out! Blizzard a-comin'! Death around the corner! Look out!"

Byron mumbled my name and I turned around to see why his voice sounded so funny. As soon as I looked at him Byron blasted me in the face with a mouthful of snow.

Man! It was hard to believe how much stuff By could put in his mouth! Him and Buphead just about died laughing as I stood there with snow and spit and ice dripping off of my face.

Byron caught his breath and said, "Aww, man, you flunked! You done so good, then you go and flunk the Blowin' Snow section of How to Survive a Blizzard, you forgot to put your hands up! What you say, Buphead, F?"

"Yeah, double F-minus!"

It was a good thing my face was numb from the cold

already or I might have froze to death. I was too embarrassed about getting tricked to tell on them so I went in the house and watched TV.

So as me and By scraped the ice off the Brown Bomber I wasn't going to get fooled again. I kept on chopping ice off the back window and ignored By's mumbling voice.

The next time I took a little rest Byron was still calling my name but sounding like he had something in his mouth. He was saying, "Keh-ee! Keh-ee! Hel' . . . hel' . . . !" When he started banging on the door of the car I went to take a peek at what was going on.

By was leaned over the outside mirror, looking at something in it real close. Big puffs of steam were coming out of the side of the mirror.

I picked up a big, hard chunk of ice to get ready for Byron's trick.

"Keh-ee! Keh-ee! Hel' me! Hel' me! Go geh Momma! Go geh Mom-ma! Huwwy uh!"

"I'm not playing, Byron! I'm not that stupid! You'd better start doing your side of the car or I'll tear you up with this iceball."

He banged his hand against the car harder and started stomping his feet. "Oh, please, Keh-ee! Hel' me, go geh Mom-ma!"

I raised the ice chunk over my head. "I'm not playing, By, you better get busy or I'm telling Dad."

I moved closer and when I got right next to him I could see boogers running out of his nose and tears running down his cheeks. These weren't tears from the cold either, these were big juicy crybaby tears! I dropped my ice chunk.

"By! What's wrong?"

"Hel' me! Keh-ee! Go geh hel'!"

I moved closer. I couldn't believe my eyes! Byron's mouth was frozen on the mirror! He was as stuck as a fly on flypaper!

I could have done a lot of stuff to him. If it had been me with my lips stuck on something like this he'd have tortured me for a couple of days before he got help. Not me, though, I nearly broke my neck trying to get into the house to rescue Byron.

As soon as I ran through the front door Momma, Dad and Joey all yelled, "Close that door!"

"Momma, quick! It's By! He's froze up outside!"

No one seemed too impressed.

I screamed, "Really! He's froze to the car! Help! He's crying!"

That shook them up. You could cut Byron's head off and he probably wouldn't cry.

"Kenneth Bernard Watson, what on earth are you talking about?"

"Momma, please hurry up!"

Momma, Dad and Joey threw on some extra coats and followed me to the Brown Bomber.

The fly was still stuck and buzzing. "Oh, Mom-ma! Hel' me! Geh me offa 'ere!"

"Oh my Lord!" Momma screamed, and I thought

she was going to do one of those movie-style faints, she even put her hand over her forehead and staggered back a little bit.

Joey, of course, started crying right along with Byron.

Dad was doing his best not to explode laughing. Big puffs of smoke were coming out of his nose and mouth as he tried to squeeze his laughs down. Finally he put his head on his arms and leaned against the car's hood and howled.

"Byron," Momma said, gently wiping tears off his cheeks with the end of her scarf, "it's O.K., sweetheart, how'd this happen?" She sounded like she was going to be crying in a minute herself.

Dad raised his head and said, "Why are you asking how it happened? Can't you tell, Wilona? This little knucklehead was kissing his reflection in the mirror and got his lips stuck!" Dad took a real deep breath. "Is your tongue stuck too?"

"No! Quit teasin', Da-ee! Hel'! Hel'!"

"Well, at least the boy hadn't gotten too passionate with himself!" Dad thought that was hilarious and put his head back on his arms.

Momma didn't see anything funny. "Daniel Watson! What are we gonna do?